STAR WARS

JEDI APPRENTICE

Special Edition

Deceptions

Jude Watson

LUCAS
BOOKS

SCHOLASTIC INC.

New York Toronto London Auckland Sydney
Mexico City New Delhi Hong Kong

ISBN 0-439-13938-4

12 11 10 9 8 7 6 5 4 3 2   1 2 3 4 5 6/0

Printed in the U.S.A.
First Scholastic printing, July 2001

CHAPTER 1

The water was cool and green. Light trickled down and made shifting patterns on the bottom. Ripples of gentle waves were formed from the force of the waterfall hitting the surface high above.

Obi-Wan Kenobi followed the shimmering tunic of his friend Bant, who swam ahead. He was wearing a breathing tube, but she was not. As a Mon Calamari, she could stay underwater for long periods of time. Bant navigated the deep pool with grace and ease.

There had been a time when he hadn't enjoyed swimming with Bant that much. He had felt clumsy in the water next to her. He hadn't liked that she was better at something. But his Master, Qui-Gon Jinn, had taught him that to value a friend's better ability was to be a true friend. Once Obi-Wan realized that, he had looked forward to their swims as much as Bant.

Bant turned and smiled at him, her arms waving softly. It was always amazing to Obi-Wan that Bant could feel so peaceful in this pool. It was here that she had almost died, chained to the bottom by the evil Xanatos. Yet here was where she always chose to swim. She *wanted* to remember, she told Obi-Wan. The day she had felt her life ebb was the day she had felt closest to the Force.

Bant pointed to the surface, and Obi-Wan nodded. They burst upward into the bright sunlight. They knew the sun was artificial, created by vast illumination banks overhead, but they welcomed its warmth on their cool skin.

Obi-Wan hauled himself up on the grassy bank facing the waterfall. Although Bant found peace in this place, he did not. Here he had battled the former Jedi student Bruck Chun for Bant's life. Here he had seen Bruck fall to his death. It had not been his fault that Bruck had died, but he still felt responsible.

"Thank you for coming here," Bant told him. "I know it is hard for you." A glint of mischief lit her eyes. "Maybe I ask you to do it because I know that."

He nudged her with a shoulder. "Oh, am I your Padawan now?"

Bant's gaze clouded, and Obi-Wan realized he

had made a mistake. He had reminded her of what they had come here to forget.

"I'm sorry," he said quietly. "I didn't mean —"

"Don't be silly." Bant hugged her knees. "I have to face my disappointment. Didn't you come here to talk to me about it?"

Bant had been hoping to be accepted by Jedi Master Tahl as her Padawan. Tahl had seemed to take a special interest in Bant, giving her projects to do and tracking her progress. Yet just yesterday, Tahl had taken off on a mission and told Yoda and the Council that she had decided to take no Padawan at all. Obi-Wan knew that Bant was upset by Tahl's decision.

"Yes," Obi-Wan admitted. "I know how it feels to be rejected. Even though Qui-Gon took me as Padawan in the end, he said no at first, and it hurt."

"I don't think there is any hope that Tahl will change her mind," Bant said sadly.

"There are other Masters," Obi-Wan said gently. "You have done well as a student. You will get the Master you were meant to have."

Bant brooded as she stared at the green water. "Yes, I know that is Jedi wisdom. But what do you do when you feel it is wrong? I felt so strongly that Tahl was the right Master. Do you know what I mean, Obi-Wan? Didn't you have the same feeling about Qui-Gon?"

"I did," Obi-Wan admitted. He did not know what to tell Bant. Jedi students were taught to trust their feelings. They were also instructed to be certain that those feelings were pure. That meant that a feeling could have more to do with what you *wished* could be, rather than what was *meant* to be. The feeling must rise in you like something that breaks loose from a deep place and floats to the surface, where it touches the sun.

Was Bant's feeling like that? He couldn't say. He could only trust his friend's judgment.

"Then maybe it's meant to be," Obi-Wan said.

"Still, I must not wait for it," Bant said. "I know that much."

Obi-Wan spied the tall form of his Master, Qui-Gon Jinn, approaching along the winding path to the pool. He stood in expectation.

Bant rose as well. "I have stolen Obi-Wan's time away from you," she said to Qui-Gon as he walked up. "I'm sorry. I needed his counsel."

Qui-Gon gave Bant the special warm smile he reserved for her. "I'm glad Obi-Wan has you as a friend, Bant. You may take all the time you wish. But right now, the Council requests Obi-Wan's presence."

"The Council?" Obi-Wan asked in apprehension. Being summoned by the entire Council was an unusual event. In Obi-Wan's experience, it was never good. Bant gave him a concerned look.

Qui-Gon nodded. "Dry yourself off, Padawan, and come. They want us immediately."

Obi-Wan quickly toweled off his hair and buckled his utility belt. He wished he had time to change into a fresh tunic. He hadn't done anything wrong . . . lately. Why did he suddenly feel as though he had?

CHAPTER 2

Obi-Wan and Qui-Gon stood in the center of the round Council Room. A steady rain beat against the windows that offered a panoramic view of the busy space lanes of Coruscant.

Qui-Gon had noted Obi-Wan's nervousness and now was proud of the way his Padawan stood, erect and seemingly at ease in front of the scrutiny of so many Council Masters. Only Qui-Gon knew how nervous Obi-Wan really was. He had faced the Council before. His Padawan had reason to be apprehensive. He knew how firm the Jedi Masters could be.

As usual, Mace Windu opened the meeting. He always looked grave, but today Qui-Gon sensed an uncharacteristic disquiet. He had hoped that this sudden summons meant that the Council had decided to send them on a special mission. But now he feared there was something wrong.

"Do not be nervous, Obi-Wan," Mace Windu said, fixing him with an intent gaze. "You are not here to be reprimanded."

It was unusual for Mace Windu to reassure anyone. Qui-Gon's concern shot up a notch. He glanced at Yoda, but he could never tell what Yoda was thinking. He turned his quick gaze to Adi Gallia. Her bearing was as regal as ever, but her eyes were full of compassion for Obi-Wan.

Mace Windu placed his hands on the arms of his chair. "We have received a communication from Vox Chun, Bruck Chun's father."

Obi-Wan gave a start. Qui-Gon was just as surprised.

"He has recently been pardoned of his crimes against the state on Telos," Mace Windu continued. "Now he wishes to come to the Temple to receive a report on the death of his son. This is his right, and the Council has agreed."

Obi-Wan nodded. His skin had gone pale. "I must speak with him?" he asked.

"You must relate the details of the death of his son, yes," Mace Windu said in a voice that held a rare gentle quality.

"Know we do that this is not easy for you, Obi-Wan," Yoda said.

"He arrives in two days," Mace Windu said. "Qui-Gon will be by your side. May the Force be with you."

They were dismissed. Qui-Gon and Obi-Wan bowed, turned, and walked from the room. As soon as the door slid shut behind them, Obi-Wan's step faltered.

"Must I do this?" he asked Qui-Gon.

"You know the answer to that question," Qui-Gon said. "I know this will be hard. But I feel it could be helpful, Padawan. You will have to speak of something you think you cannot, something deep in your heart. Perhaps if you see this thing plain and honest in front of you, it will cease to plague your dreams."

Obi-Wan gave him a startled glance.

"Yes, I know how much it still troubles you," Qui-Gon said gently. "Isn't it time to put an end to it?"

Obi-Wan's face was still drawn. Qui-Gon put a hand on his shoulder. "Find Bant and get some food. It is past time for the midday meal." Food always revived Obi-Wan somewhat. Qui-Gon did not want the boy to worry too much about the upcoming interview. No doubt it would be rough, but Obi-Wan was in the right, and so he would survive it.

After Obi-Wan headed for the turbolift, Qui-Gon lingered outside the Council Room. He hoped to have a talk with Yoda. Tahl's decision not to take a Padawan and her sudden disappearance troubled him. It was always helpful to have Yoda's perspective.

The door slid open noiselessly, and the Council members filed out. Yoda spotted him and nodded. Qui-Gon had an idea that Yoda knew exactly why he was waiting.

"Worried you are, Qui-Gon," Yoda said as he walked toward him, his robe rocking with his sideways gait. "Yet not just about your Padawan, I think."

"Tahl," Qui-Gon said shortly. "Why did she not take a Padawan? And why did she leave so suddenly?"

Yoda leaned on his staff. "Should I be the one you ask this?"

Qui-Gon sighed. "You mean I should ask Tahl. I wanted your opinion first."

Yoda nodded. "Think I do that Tahl did not want to burden Bant with a blind Master. Afraid she was that it would limit Bant's experience."

"Burden! Limits!" Qui-Gon exclaimed incredulously. He could not associate those words with Tahl. "That's ridiculous!"

"Yet not think so, Tahl does. Time she needs, Qui-Gon. Help her with this, you cannot. Her decision, it is." Yoda's wise gaze rested on Qui-Gon. "And time it was she left the Temple to take on wider duties. We sent her to the pilot program on Centax 2."

Qui-Gon was surprised. Centax 2 was a satellite of Coruscant. Transports and spaceliners often docked there in order to ferry goods and passengers to Coruscant on smaller ships. The Jedi had chosen Centax 2 to set up their new pilot program, run by Jedi Knight Clee Rhara.

"Is there a problem?" Qui-Gon asked.

"That we do not know," Yoda answered, blinking his large eyes. "We only suspect. Aware you are that this project does not have the full support of the Council. Clee Rhara believes that the Jedi should have a squad of starfighter pilots. Some agree. Some do not."

Qui-Gon knew the project was controversial. The Council had finally agreed to the operation, but only on a trial basis. Some of the gifted older students, like Obi-Wan's friend Garen Muln, had been chosen for it. There were some on the Council who believed that Jedi should continue to take rides on consular ships or haulers, or borrow small transports for short flights. They believed that Jedi pilots would lead to a Jedi fleet, a complex operation that would divert their attention from peacekeeping efforts in the galaxy.

"Clee Rhara, you know," Yoda said. "Charismatic, she is. A following among the young pilots, she has. Many are delaying their Padawan status. Allow this, the Council does, but many are uneasy."

Qui-Gon nodded. He had gone through

Temple training with Clee Rhara. She had a bright wit and a fierce will that had attracted followers even then.

"What is Tahl's mission there?" Qui-Gon asked curiously.

"A grave problem we have," Yoda said. "Until now, the Senate donated the starfighters for Jedi pilots. Outmoded or damaged, the starfighters are. Clee Rhara has her own shipyard for refitting. Worked well, this system has. But mechanical failures lately there have been. One quite serious. A Coruscant air taxi was almost hit. Aboard, an important Senator was."

"Does Clee Rhara suspect sabotage?" Qui-Gon asked.

Yoda nodded. "Tahl has gone to investigate. Some there are in the Senate who resent the Jedi. Whispers there are about our taking advantage. Track these whispers, we cannot. Concerned, the Council is. Clee Rhara must make the program work, or abandon it we must."

"I see," Qui-Gon said. "So if Tahl can discover that the ships were sabotaged, the program can continue."

"Perhaps." Yoda straightened and began to move toward the turbolift. "Watching us some in the Senate are. Hoping to see us fail, per-

haps. And watching they will be the investigation of Bruck's death. Also, forget we should not
that Vox Chun was once in the employ of one
who plotted to destroy us."

"Xanatos," Qui-Gon said. His former Padawan
was dead. Yet the evil he spread lived on.

CHAPTER 3

Qui-Gon decided that the most courteous thing would be to meet Vox Chun at the landing platform as he arrived. Obi-Wan knew his Master was right, but he wished he could postpone seeing Bruck's father for a while longer.

"Here he comes." Qui-Gon indicated a silver transport heading toward them. He eyed the sleek lines of the ship. "How does someone who just got out of jail afford a transport like that? Perhaps Vox still has powerful friends."

Obi-Wan was too nervous to answer. Moments later, the transport glided to a stop, and the ramp lowered and the exit door slid open. A figure stood at the top. Obi-Wan gasped. It was Bruck.

He took a step backward, and Qui-Gon put a hand on his arm. "No," Qui-Gon told him in a fierce undertone. "It is not him, Obi-Wan. The boy only looks like Bruck."

The boy had a shock of white hair, like Bruck. He was dressed in a rough tunic similar to a Jedi's. But as he descended, Obi-Wan began to breathe again. He saw that the boy's features were softer and that he was a few years younger than Obi-Wan.

"A brother," Qui-Gon murmured. "They wanted to unsettle us. That is why he went first."

Behind the boy, Vox Chun walked slowly down the ramp, his deep purple cloak swirling around the tops of his boots. The last passenger followed a step or two behind, and Obi-Wan glanced at him curiously. Vox Chun had not indicated that he was bringing anyone with him, and the Jedi had assumed he was coming alone. This man was shorter than Obi-Wan. He could be Qui-Gon's age, or he could be older. It was impossible to tell. He had a smooth, unlined face and dark hair cut short. He wore an austere black jacket and trousers.

Qui-Gon nodded as the three approached. "Welcome to the Jedi Temple. I am Qui-Gon Jinn, and this is my Padawan, Obi-Wan Kenobi."

Vox Chun's eyes were the same blue-frost color as Bruck's. They slid over Obi-Wan like a coating of ice over water. He returned Qui-Gon's nod of greeting. "I am Vox Chun, and this is my son, Kad Chun. This is a family friend, Sano Sauro. He has come to give us emotional support."

Obi-Wan glanced at Sano Sauro. His opaque black gaze and severe, expressionless manner gave no hint of his feelings. Obi-Wan couldn't imagine going to him for anything involving emotions.

"This way," Qui-Gon said, indicating the passage into the Temple. "We have refreshments waiting, if you —"

"I've come for answers, not for tea," Vox Chun said brusquely.

"Fine. We have prepared a conference room —"

"Take me to the place where my son was killed."

Qui-Gon bristled at his choice of words, but answered carefully. "You may see where your son died."

Obi-Wan trailed after Kad. From behind, the boy's stocky build and stance brought Bruck back to Obi-Wan vividly. Bruck had been a bully who had tormented Obi-Wan during his years at the Temple. For some reason, Obi-Wan had gotten under his skin. He did not have any good memories of the boy.

Yet Bruck had developed a close core of friends at the Temple. He had inspired loyalty.

There had been a side of him that Obi-Wan hadn't seen. That was what tormented Obi-Wan. There must have been good in Bruck.

They did not speak in the turbolift or during the walk through the corridors to the Room of a Thousand Fountains. Usually, visitors were immediately struck with a peaceful feeling as they entered the vast space filled with fragrant greenery and hidden trickling fountains. The air smelled fresh and cool. Kad stopped for a moment, but Vox pushed him along. Sano Sauro's dour expression did not change.

"Let us begin," Vox Chun said abruptly. "How exactly did my son die?"

"The Temple had been under siege from an unknown assailant," Qui-Gon began. "We knew that your son was involved —"

"I am not interested in your Jedi history," Vox Chun interrupted rudely. "I want to know facts." He turned to Obi-Wan. "Where did you engage with him? Who drew his lightsaber first?"

"I followed him here from outside the Council Room," Obi-Wan said. "We both already had our lightsabers drawn."

"You mean your lightsaber magically appeared in your hand? You did not draw it in attack or defense?" Vox Chun asked sarcastically.

"I drew it when Xanatos and Bruck came

through the vent outside the Council Room," Obi-Wan said.

"Did Bruck have his lightsaber drawn?"

"No," Obi-Wan answered. "He was hiding in a vent, waiting to steal —"

"Jedi history," Vox interrupted, waving his hand. "Not relevant to my question. So he drew his lightsaber when he saw yours?"

"Yes," Obi-Wan said. "We battled, and Xanatos ordered him to go make sure Bant was dead. He ran, and I followed."

"Did you attack him from behind?"

"No, he turned and came at me. We fought. We ended up near the fountain."

"Show me this fountain."

Obi-Wan led the way down the winding paths to the thundering waterfall and deep green pool.

"The waterfall was not operating at the time, since the Temple systems had been shut down," he explained. "But there was water in the pool. I saw Bant chained to the bottom. Her eyes were closed. She was alive, but barely. We fought all the way up that hill," Obi-Wan said, pointing to the rocky slope. "When we got to the top, I realized that in a few seconds all the water systems would be reactivated in the Temple. They had been shut down because of a bug Xanatos had planted in the system. I drove Bruck into the dry waterfall bed. My plan was that when the water came back on, Bruck's lightsaber would short out. That would disarm him, and I could then free Bant."

"And leave your enemy standing?" Vox Chun asked. "That does not sound like a Jedi warrior."

"On the contrary," Qui-Gon broke in. "We avoid death at all cost. To disarm our opponent is our first objective."

Vox Chun shrugged, as if Qui-Gon had just spouted empty words. "Obviously, this plan did not work out," he said evenly to Obi-Wan.

"His lightsaber did short out," Obi-Wan said. "He was knee-deep in water. He scrambled to get his footing nearer the bank, where the rocks are. He picked them up and began to throw them at me. In his struggle to get the rocks, he went too close to the edge of the waterfall. The rocks are very slippery there." Obi-Wan paused. His throat felt dry. "The current was pushing him. He lost his balance. I reached out a hand . . . it was too late. He fell below and hit his head. I ran down. I checked his vital signs, but he was already dead. He died as soon as he hit, I am sure. He did not . . . suffer."

"So that is your story," Vox Chun said.

"It is the truth," Obi-Wan said quietly.

"We are leaving now." Vox turned to go. Kad

and Sano Sauro followed. Then Sano Sauro turned back and fixed his dark, opaque gaze on Obi-Wan.

"In your opinion, did Bruck Chun really intend to kill Bant?" he asked softly.

"Xanatos ordered him to," Obi-Wan replied.

"That does not answer my question. Did Bruck intend to kill Bant?"

"I believe he did."

"You believe or you know?"

"I . . . believe."

"What do you *know*? Did he take any action to kill Bant?"

"He didn't have to! She was chained under-water!"

"A Mon Calamari underwater is not so un-usual."

"She was almost out of her store of oxygen."

"You know this? Or is this something you be-lieve?"

"I know it. She told me so after I rescued her."

Sauro nodded thoughtfully. "How do you know that Bruck would not have dived down and saved her himself, if more time had gone by?"

Obi-Wan stared at him. How could he know the answer to that question? He didn't think Bruck would have saved Bant. But that was what he *believed*. He didn't *know*.

Sauro waited, but when Obi-Wan said nothing, he gave his first smile. It made Obi-Wan shiver.

He turned back to Vox Chun. "I'm ready."

"There is one last thing," Qui-Gon said. "The Jedi would like to present you with this, with our sorrow. Bruck was one of us, and we mourn him."

He reached into his tunic and withdrew the hilt of Bruck's lightsaber. The crystals had been removed, but the hilt still bore the markings Bruck had carved. Qui-Gon bowed and presented it to Vox Chun.

Vox Chun shoved it in his tunic pocket without looking at it. Then he turned and walked off without saying good-bye. Kad Chun and Sano Sauro followed.

With a glance, Qui-Gon told Obi-Wan that he would show the visitors out. Obi-Wan could remain.

As soon as they were out of sight, Obi-Wan sank onto the soft grass of the bank. He felt emptied out and light-headed, as though he'd been sick with a fever.

He had told the truth, and they had not believed him. He tried to take comfort in the fact that at least it was over.

Yet deep inside he feared that it was only beginning.

CHAPTER 4

Qui-Gon watched Vox Chun's sleek transport rise in the sky. The meeting had not gone well. In fact, it could not have gone worse.

He had seen in Obi-Wan's face that meeting Vox and Kad Chun had only increased his feelings of guilt. Yet guilt must ease for Obi-Wan so that sorrow could take its place.

He had spoken to the boy, but the words had not reached him. *Life* needed to teach him. Time. Experience. These he could not hand over like a piece of advice.

But he could do something for his Padawan. He could distract him.

Obi-Wan had returned to his quarters. He lay on his sleep-couch, staring at the ceiling.

Qui-Gon leaned against the door frame. "How would you like to take an excursion to Centax 2?"

Obi-Wan sat up. His troubled look vanished. "Really? I can see Garen! And those starfighters!"

"Yes, I thought you would like that. Tahl is investigating some problems there. I thought she might be able to use our help."

Obi-Wan gave a vigorous nod. He would do anything for Tahl. "When do we start?"

"Now, if you like," Qui-Gon said. "Get your gear together. We can take an air taxi there."

Obi-Wan grabbed his survival pack, and they headed for the landing platform. There, they boarded an air taxi. It was a short flight to the upper atmosphere, where Centax 2 was located. The satellite was a small, bluish moon with no vegetation or water. Its deep valleys and mountain ranges had been leveled in order to accommodate huge landing platforms and various tech support buildings and hangars.

The landing platforms were busy with traffic, and the air taxi joined a line waiting to dock. At last they were given clearance to land. They exited the air taxi, and Qui-Gon led the way to a covered moving walkway that had exits for different landing platforms. They got off at the very end, where the walkway looped around to return. Then they trudged along a windswept lane to a small, private landing area in the distance. Obi-Wan could see five starfighters lined up outside a tech dome.

As he got closer, he saw two starfighters zooming overhead, just silver streaks in the sky. He kept his eyes on them as they dove, screaming, toward the surface, then pulled up. They flew side by side in mirror formation, then broke apart.

"I wish I could learn to fly like that," Obi-Wan said admiringly.

After the two starfighters landed, Obi-Wan recognized a familiar figure jumping out of one of the cockpits. Garen Muln removed his helmet and shook out a head of thick, shoulder-length hair. To Obi-Wan's surprise, Garen no longer wore the short hair and long braid of a senior Temple student. He saw that the other pilot had grown his hair as well.

Garen's keen gaze picked out the two figures approaching. After only a few seconds, he recognized Obi-Wan. With a delighted shout, he leaped off the starfighter and ran toward him.

"Obi-Wan! Why didn't you tell me you were coming? It's so good to see you!" Garen collected himself as he realized he had neglected to greet a Jedi Master. "Excuse me, Qui-Gon Jinn," he said, bowing. "Welcome."

Qui-Gon smiled. "Obi-Wan and I decided to see how you were doing here at the base."

"We're doing great. Except for a few mishaps lately, but Clee Rhara has straightened that all out."

Qui-Gon raised an eyebrow, but said nothing.

"Just wait until you meet her," Garen told Obi-Wan, his eyes shining. "She's incredible. The best pilot I've ever seen. She's got us doing things in the air we only dreamed about. I've come such a long way from the Temple!"

"You don't look like a Jedi any longer," Obi-Wan said, noting Garen's flight coveralls and long hair.

"I'm still a Jedi, don't worry," Garen said, flashing a grin.

Just then Clee Rhara strode out from the tech dome. She was dressed in flight coveralls, just like Garen. Her bright orange hair was untamed and flew around her face in the wind. Clee Rhara was petite and slender, barely coming up to Qui-Gon's shoulder, but her compact body was built of wiry muscle. She saw Qui-Gon, and a broad smile broke out on her face.

"What a surprise!" she called, hurrying forward.

"I'd like you to meet my Padawan, Obi-Wan Kenobi."

Obi-Wan was examined by a pair of intense eyes the same color as Clee's vibrant orange hair. "I've heard good things about you from Garen," Clee said. "Welcome." She linked her arms with Obi-Wan and Qui-Gon. "Let me show you the outfit. And Tahl is here. She'll be thrilled that you've come."

Clee gave them a tour, showing them the re-tooled starfighters, the student quarters, the study rooms, hangars, and even the kitchens. Qui-Gon noted how the gaze of the Jedi students followed Clee as she strolled the grounds. Obviously she inspired great loyalty.

Clee ended her tour at the tech center, where her students had hands-on experience with engines and hyperdrives. Tahl sat at a utility desk, using a voice-activated computer. She stopped speaking as they walked in.

"You'll never guess who —" Clee began.

"Qui-Gon." Tahl said his name flatly. Qui-Gon felt a flicker of apprehension. Tahl had never greeted him so coolly.

If Clee noticed Tahl's manner, she made no sign of it. "Here we are, the three of us, all together again!" she said cheerfully.

"Yes," Tahl said.

Qui-Gon shot Clee a look. They hadn't seen each other in years, but their old friendship gave them a connection that would never weaken. She knew immediately that he wanted to talk to Tahl alone.

"Obi-Wan, do you want to see the starships?" Clee asked.

"Yes!" Obi-Wan answered immediately.

"Come on, Garen and I will show you the fleet," Clee said, striding toward the door. "Then we'll head back for the evening meal. See you there, Qui-Gon."

Qui-Gon waited until the others had left. He did not approach Tahl. "You're angry that I came."

She turned away from him so that he could not read the expression on her lovely face. Sometimes she did this so that he would not have an advantage.

"You think I am in need of help. You think I cannot handle a mission alone."

Qui-Gon was about to insist that such a statement was ridiculous, but he stopped himself. He did not need to see Tahl's face to realize that she was feeling vulnerable. The act of choosing a Padawan had pushed her up against something deep inside that hurt her, that made her doubt herself. He knew that feeling well, for different reasons.

"No," he said. "I came because Obi-Wan had a hard time with Vox Chun. I am worried about him. I knew he would enjoy seeing the base. If we could help out as well, it might distract him further."

"Ah," Tahl said mockingly, "and that is the *only* reason you came?"

"I heard that you had decided not to take a Padawan —"

"And you thought I might need a heart-to-heart talk." Tahl whipped her face around again. He read lines of bitterness there. "You want to tell me how reluctant you were to take a Padawan, how much it cost you, how valuable it has turned out to be, how I must realize that even though I am blind I have much to give to an apprentice. Do you think I don't know every word you would say? So please refrain. Any discussion of Padawans or Bant is off-limits. I mean it, Qui-Gon."

"All right," he said quietly. "But will you, as a favor to me and Obi-Wan, let us help you in your investigation?"

"Just know that I do it for Obi-Wan."

"Fair enough." He walked closer and drew up a chair next to her. "What do you have so far?"

"My contacts in the Senate tell me that there are rumors that Clee Rhara sabotaged the ships herself," Tahl said, passing a weary hand over her eyes.

"Why would she do that?" Qui-Gon asked, startled.

"In order to prove to the Senate that the project needs funding and more up-to-date ships," Tahl said.

Clee's booming indignation suddenly echoed

off the metal walls of the tech dome. "What a load of sludge oil!" She strode toward them, her hands on her hips. "I would never endanger my pilots!"

"I thought you were giving Obi-Wan a tour of the starfighters," Qui-Gon said.

"I came back to make sure you two weren't killing each other," Clee said. "I remember how you used to scrap at the Temple."

"We are Jedi Knights now," Qui-Gon said. "We don't scrap."

Tahl smiled. "We argue, and then I win."

Clee flopped in a chair. "Well, I'm glad to see both of you. I'm really in a mess. If I don't figure out who is sabotaging my fleet, I'm sure the Council will cancel the whole program. I can't let that happen!"

"Tell me about security," Qui-Gon said.

"Ships are refitted at a nearby yard, and all the workers have undergone Senate security checks. After the first incident, I restricted the workers who take care of Jedi ships to two. It slows things down, but it's safer. Each of them has passed the highest level of security clearance from the Senate. I thought everything would be fine. Yet another incident happened after this."

"So it has to be one of the two workers," Qui-Gon said.

"Or someone is finding a way to sneak into a highly restricted area," Tahl said.

Clee leaned forward and gripped her hands in frustration. "I can't tighten security more than I already have. Those Senate security checks are incredibly thorough."

"There's another possibility," Qui-Gon said. "Someone in the Senate is behind this, and one or both of the security clearances is false."

"I didn't think of that," Tahl said. "That would explain the rumors in the Senate. The same someone could be responsible. Someone who wants this project to fail."

"But why?" Clee asked. "Who would object to a handful of Jedi Temple students learning how to fly starfighters?"

"Someone who is afraid of the Jedi increasing their power," Qui-Gon mused. "The program is still young. Its potential may scare them."

Qui-Gon's comlink signaled, and he excused himself to answer it, walking a few paces away. It was Yoda.

"Unhappy news I have," Yoda said without preliminaries. "Ruled the Senate has to form a subcommittee to investigate Bruck's death. Vox Chun has a hidden powerful ally there. Discovered we have that Sano Sauro is a prosecutor. Rumor is he is hungry to make his mark.

Return you must, Qui-Gon. Three witnesses there will be — yourself, Bant, and Obi-Wan. Fear I do that this process will take its toll on your Padawan."

Qui-Gon's heart sank. "Yes," he said softly. "I fear it will as well."

CHAPTER 5

The hearing committee of the Senate did not waste time. They called the Jedi to their private inquiry room the very next day.

Obi-Wan felt a sense of dread as he dressed that morning. He could barely choke down his morning meal. He was almost relieved when it was time to meet Qui-Gon and head for the Senate.

"There will be fifteen Senators on the panel," Qui-Gon explained to Bant and Obi-Wan as they threaded their way through the Senate's lavender halls. The hallways were thronged with Senators striding by importantly, with scurrying aides, consorts, and droids at their heels.

"I will be called first," Qui-Gon explained. "Then Bant. Obi-Wan will be last. Sano Sauro will try to twist your words, so be sure you speak the truth with every sentence you utter. The Jedi have elected not to use a representative. We have truth on our side. Remember that."

Obi-Wan nodded. Qui-Gon's calm gaze was reassuring. The walls of the Inquiry Room were fashioned from transparisteel, so Obi-Wan could see that the Senators had already gathered at the long table inside. It was set up on a platform. Vox Chun, Kad Chun, and Sano Sauro were already sitting opposite them. An empty table waited for the Jedi.

"Senator Pi T'Egal is the head of the commit-tee," Qui-Gon said softly, indicating the Senator who sat at the center of the table. "That is good. He is a friend of the Jedi."

The transparisteel doors slid open. Qui-Gon, Obi-Wan, and Bant gave short bows to the Senators. Then they took their places at the empty table.

"If we are all here, we can begin," Pi T'Egal said. He pressed a button and the transparisteel walls turned opaque. Obi-Wan had expected the shift, but it made him feel suddenly trapped.

Find your calm center. He struggled to breathe as Pi T'Egal consulted his datapad and pressed a few buttons. Bant's fingers gently squeezed Obi-Wan's forearm in support.

At last Pi T'Egal looked up. "This is not a crim-inal trial," he said. "It is an inquiry only. Vox and Kad Chun have asked for a full accounting of the death of Bruck Chun in the Jedi Temple. We Senators have agreed to rule whether the death was by mischance or if Obi-Wan Kenobi bears some measure of responsibility for this. If our ruling is deliberate intent or responsibility, Vox and Kad Chun can then pursue the matter in the criminal courts of Coruscant. Does everyone understand this?"

Everyone nodded.

Pi T'Egal turned to Vox Chun. "Do you understand that if we find there is no responsibility by others for your son's death you cannot pursue this further?"

"I do," Vox Chun said.

"Then let us begin. The first witness will be the Jedi Knight Qui-Gon Jinn."

Qui-Gon rose and went to a chair set up on the platform, angled so that all the Senators could see him clearly.

"Please inform us of the events leading up to and surrounding the death of Bruck Chun."

Qui-Gon began easily, quickly sketching the problems the Temple had been experiencing and the fact that there was an intruder on the grounds.

"We knew that Bruck Chun was involved in the petty thefts," he said. "He disappeared, and we also knew that a more powerful figure had intercepted security. We assumed that

Bruck Chun had smuggled this being into the Temple."

"You did not know this as a fact," Sano Sauro interrupted.

"No," Qui-Gon said, his cool gaze resting on the attorney. "That is why I used the word 'assumed.'"

"Please go on, Qui-Gon Jinn," Pi T'Egal said.

Qui-Gon outlined the many instances of sabotage, including the attack on Yoda and the sabotage of a horizontal turbolift that had trapped a dozen small children and their caretaker. Then he explained how they discovered that their adversary was his former Padawan, Xanatos, who was then head of the giant mining corporation, Offworld. They trapped Xanatos and Bruck outside the Jedi Council room as the two burst through an overhead vent.

"I knocked Bruck's lightsaber from his hand," Qui-Gon said quietly. "Xanatos grabbed the boy and held the lightsaber to his neck."

Sano Sauro sat up straighter. "So Xanatos threatened the boy? Bruck Chun was his prisoner, not his accomplice?"

"No," Qui-Gon said. "Xanatos felt loyalty to no one. He was willing to endanger Bruck's life in order to gain an advantage."

"Such is your belief," Sano Sauro sneered.

"Yes. Based on many encounters with Xanatos, I have come to see how he reacts under pressure," Qui-Gon answered. "We were able to force Xanatos to push Bruck aside. Bruck was able to recover his lightsaber. Xanatos told him to go to Bant and make sure she was dead."

Pi T'Egal leaned forward. "He said those words?"

"'Make sure she is dead,'" Qui-Gon quoted. "Those words exactly."

"Did you instruct Obi-Wan to kill Bruck?" Sano Sauro demanded.

Qui-Gon's hands gripped the chair arm for a moment, the only sign that the insolence in Sauro's voice had reached him. "No. Jedi do not instruct to kill. My instruction was to follow Bruck in order to prevent him from killing Bant. This is exactly what he did. I mourn the loss of life, but I am proud of my Padawan's actions." Qui-Gon gave Obi-Wan a warm glance.

"Proud?" Sano Sauro stood. "Proud that a young Jedi student is dead?"

"Proud that Obi-Wan tried his best to save him, even after Bruck Chun tried very hard to kill him," Qui-Gon said, his voice strong. "Proud that he was able to show mercy and compassion even while facing great anger from another. That is the Jedi way."

Sano Sauro sat with a sneer. "Did you see this . . . *compassion* for yourself, Qui-Gon Jinn?"

"No. I was engaged in a battle with Xanatos."

"Then we will have to take your word for it."

"No," Qui-Gon said. "You will have to take Obi-Wan's word for it. I do."

Sano Sauro waved his hand. "I have no more questions for this witness."

Pi T'Egal looked at the other Senators. None of them had questions. "Thank you, Qui-Gon Jinn. Now let us hear from Bant."

Qui-Gon strode back to the table, giving Bant an encouraging look on the way. Bant came forward. Her salmon skin glowed, but her eyes were dim with nervousness. When she sat, Obi-Wan saw how she reached down inside to calm herself. Her chin lifted, and she turned a resolute face to Pi T'Egal.

Pi T'Egal spoke gently, for Bant inspired gentleness in everyone. "Tell us what happened that afternoon, Bant."

"I was captured by Xanatos and Bruck Chun," Bant said in a clear, steady voice. "They took me to the Room of a Thousand Fountains. We used the water tunnels so that we would not be seen. There, Xanatos chained me to the bottom of the waterfall pool. He told me to prepare for death, that Obi-Wan and Qui-Gon would not be able to save me. I did not believe him. But as the time went on, I realized that I had reached the limit of how long I could stay underwater. Then I went beyond it. I knew I was close to death. I prepared for it. And then I felt Obi-Wan's presence. I could not see him, but I knew he was there. I felt the Force surge and give me strength to hold on. A short time later, I felt Obi-Wan release me and carry me to the surface. He dragged me up onto the bank. I saw Bruck Chun lying nearby. He was dead."

Bant concluded in a soft voice and bowed her head. "That is all I know."

The note of insolence in Sano Sauro's voice changed to the soft purring of a deadly animal. "You say you were near your limit underwater. Is there a prescribed amount of time a Calamarian can be without oxygen?"

"No," Bant said. "It varies from individual to individual."

"Have you ever passed out underwater, Bant?"

"No."

"Never reached your limit?"

"No," Bant said. "Not until that day."

"Yet you did not pass out, did you? How old are you, Bant?" Sano Sauro asked, suddenly switching gears.

"I am twelve. I was eleven at the time this happened."

"If you had never reached it before, and you did not reach it that day, how do you *know* you were close to death?" Sano Sauro fired the question abruptly.

She blinked slowly. "I felt death was near —"

"So it was a *feeling.*"

Obi-Wan's muscles tensed. Confusion flittered over Bant's face. She had not expected this attack.

"Jedi are taught to trust our feelings."

"Ah. And what was your state of mind?"

"I was in a meditative state, waiting for death should it choose to come."

"Can you say for sure how much longer you could have held out, if Kenobi had not rescued you?"

Bant hesitated.

"The truth," he warned.

"No . . . I cannot . . ."

Sano Sauro spun around and faced the Senators. "So we are to trust the *feeling* of an eleven-year-old that she was in mortal danger, so that any efforts to free her were justified. A young man is dead because of *this*?"

"But I know my abilities and my capacities," Bant cried. "I am sure I was close to death!"

"I have no more questions," Sano Sauro said.

"I think it's time to end for today," Pi T'Egal

announced. "We will meet again tomorrow at the same time."

The Senators rose. Bant rose shakily from the chair and approached Obi-Wan and Qui-Gon.

"I failed you. . . ."

"No," Qui-Gon said firmly. "You told the truth."

"It's all right, Bant," Obi-Wan said. "It was that Sano Sauro, twisting everything. He has no respect for Jedi."

"The Senators do," Qui-Gon told her. "They will not swallow his interpretation. Do not fret about it." He led her gently toward the door, speeding up his pace a fraction in order to avoid Vox Chun and Sano Sauro, who were also heading in that direction.

Obi-Wan was left with Kad Chun. Their eyes met. A wave of anger washed over Obi-Wan, a wave he knew he must resist. But he could not. They had attacked Bant, and he could not forgive them for that.

Kad caught his anger. Obi-Wan saw the flash of satisfaction in the pale gaze that was so like Bruck's.

"So you are not so perfect, are you, Obi-Wan Kenobi?" Kad asked in a tone of soft menace. "I see the hate in your eyes."

"I don't hate you, Kad," Obi-Wan answered,

struggling to keep his voice even. "But that attack on Bant — is that your idea of justice?"

Kad's hands balled into fists. "And killing my brother — is that your idea of mercy?" he spat out.

Their gazes locked. Obi-Wan had never faced such blazing, personal hatred and pain. He felt the shock of it hit him. He wanted to run, but he stood his ground.

Kad finally tore his gaze away. Then he turned and hurried after his father.

CHAPTER 6

There was nothing more he could do for Obi-Wan, Qui-Gon reflected as he boarded an air taxi for Centax 2. He had said everything that needed to be said. One of the hardest tasks of a Master was the decision to step back. His Padawan needed to deal with his feelings on his own.

And Tahl needed his help, whether she wanted it or not.

He landed on Centax 2 and took the moving walkway to the Jedi base. He found Tahl in the tech dome, going over starship specifications.

By now she could recognize his step moments after he entered a room.

"I thought I needed to know some details of a starship engine," she said without preliminaries. She pushed away the voice recorder that read specifications aloud to her and turned to him. "How was the hearing?"

"Hard to say." Qui-Gon sat next to her. "It was very hard on Bant."

"Bant? Why?" Tahl's tone was sharp. Qui-Gon noted how she instinctively jumped to Bant's defense.

"Sano Sauro grilled her about how long a Mon Calamari can stay underwater. Bant was forced to say that she could not be sure how close to death she was."

Tahl groaned. "And Bant would see that as a betrayal of Obi-Wan."

"I'm afraid so. I'm hoping Obi-Wan will talk to her at the Temple. Even in the midst of his own pain, he will reach out to Bant. Obi-Wan himself cannot find composure."

She sighed. "They do so much and have come so far. We can't forget they are still young."

"I know he'll be fine in the end," Qui-Gon said. "But it's hard to stand by and watch him go through this." He looked at Tahl searchingly. "Yet it is satisfying just the same to be able to stand by him."

Tahl turned and ran her fingers over a blueprint. The lines were raised so that her fingers could read the shapes, and the voice recorder told her what she was examining. "I didn't realize that the thrust dampers were located so far to the rear," she said coolly.

Obviously, even a gentle hint that Tahl could benefit from a Master/Padawan relationship would be ignored. Qui-Gon decided to follow her lead. Primarily because he knew he had no choice.

"Have you interviewed the two workers yet?" he asked.

"No, I was just about to. They know an investigator is here. I wanted them to be nervous. Do you want to come?"

"If you don't mind —"

"Of course I mind," Tahl said, rising smoothly. "But since when does that stop you?"

At least there was amusement in her tone. Qui-Gon walked beside her to the adjoining hangar, where the starfighters were refitted.

Once they got into the hangar itself, Qui-Gon had to restrain himself from taking Tahl's arm. The ground was cluttered with tools and stacks of parts, large and small. But using her extraordinary reflexes and special training, Tahl now used a gliding walk that guided her safely around obstacles.

"You do not need TooJay any longer for navigation, I see," Qui-Gon remarked, referring to Tahl's endlessly chattering personal navigation droid.

Her lips curved in a smile. "I worked very hard so that I don't. But I brought her here anyway. Unfortunately, I still need her for some things."

"The mechanics are to the left," Qui-Gon instructed.

He studied them as he and Tahl approached. One was a Twi'lek, with large head tails wrapped up in cloth to keep out of his way. His skin was light blue. The other mechanic was human, his body short and compact, the sides of his head shaved so that his close-cropped hair ran down the center of his head.

"We wonder if we could have a few words with you," Tahl said.

The two mechanics put down their tools and turned to them. "Of course," the Twi'lek said a bit nervously. "I am Haly Dura and this is Tarrence Chenati. What can we do for you?"

"We are investigating the mechanical failures on the starfighters," Qui-Gon explained.

"We already have gone through an investigation," Haly Dura said. "We were cleared."

"We just want to ask a few questions," Tahl said. "Clee Rhara has asked for our help."

"I'm sure we have answered all those questions," Haly Dura said impatiently.

"Then you will answer them a second time," Tahl said, a hard edge beneath her calm tone.

Tarrence Chenati glanced at his coworker. "Of course we will cooperate. We do not want a cloud of suspicion over our heads. We are concerned as well. We have gone over every moment of our shifts with Clee Rhara but can't understand how it could have happened."

"This is a restricted area," Haly Dura said. "We're the only ones allowed here. That means that someone must have broken in after hours."

Qui-Gon studied both mechanics. He concentrated on looks and gestures for clues that one might be lying, knowing that Tahl would pick up vocal clues.

"You do all the repair work on the starfighters, correct?" Tahl asked.

The two workers nodded, then realized Tahl could not see them.

"Yes," they said together.

"What about the ionization chamber?" Tahl asked.

The last accident had taken place because of a malfunction in the ionization chamber, Qui-Gon knew.

"The ionization chamber did not need retrofitting," Haly Dura said. "We ran a check on it, of course."

"How do you do that?" Tahl asked pleasantly.

"On the control panel. Here." Haly Dura indicated a computer panel. "It showed no problems."

"The starship was cleared for flying the next

day," Tarrence Chenati said. "Until then the ship was here, in the hangar, under tight surveillance."

"Do you mind if we look around?" Qui-Gon asked.

"Help yourself."

The two mechanics went on with their work, soldering laser power converters. Qui-Gon and Tahl strolled through the hangar.

"Did you pick up anything from our two friends?" Qui-Gon murmured.

"A smell," Tahl whispered back. "It was on Tarrence Chenati but not Haly Dura. Could be nothing. It's an industrial smell, though. I have an idea. Let's come back after they've gone."

They did not have long to wait. The two workers soon quit for the day. Clee Rhara had given the Jedi all the security codes, so they quickly slipped back inside. Qui-Gon powered up the lights. Not too long ago, he would have been leery of relying on Tahl's sense of smell for a clue. He knew better now.

Tahl seated herself on a low bench. "Qui-Gon, bring me the different compounds they use — grease, conductors, solvents — they should be all along the east wall. There's a storage unit — I know it from the schematic of the repair sector. Bring them one at a time."

Qui-Gon was too curious to mind being ordered. He found the storage unit. Everything was neatly labeled. Qui-Gon knew a fair amount about starship engines, but even he was surprised to see how many different kinds of grease, conductors, and solvents were used to keep a starship running.

He started with grease. Tahl inspected the various kinds, her eyes closed in concentration. After each deep sniff, she shook her head. Some of the chemical compounds caused her to cough violently, and her eyes streamed tears, but she kept going. They had run through eleven different chemical compounds when Qui-Gon brought her something simply labeled CONDUCTOR X-112.

Tahl took a deep sniff and let out a racking cough. She leaned over and took deep breaths of air. When she could speak, she croaked, "That's it. No wonder I could still smell it."

Qui-Gon entered the compound into the computer to find out its uses. "It only has one function — as a conductor in the ionization chamber."

Tahl slapped her hand on the bench. "That's what I was hoping for. Chenati lied. He worked on the ionization chamber. Yet they said they didn't have to."

"And that's where the malfunction was," Qui-Gon said. "Let's go back and check out Chenati's credentials again."

After frustrated hours of searching, Tahl and Qui-Gon had come up with nothing.

"Everything checks out," Tahl said, sighing. "Just because I pick up a smell from the guy's coveralls doesn't mean he's a saboteur. There's probably another explanation."

"His security checks are flawless," Qui-Gon said, looking at the information they'd amassed. "His record is incredibly clean."

"Yet he has no family. Never married or had children," Tahl mused. "And he sure moved around the galaxy."

"You could say all those things about me," Qui-Gon said.

Tahl's lips curved in a smile. "Well, you are a suspicious character."

It was close to dawn. Soon the pilots and Clee Rhara would awaken and the day would begin. Today all the starfighter pilots would take to the air.

"Maybe his clearances *are* too good," Tahl said. "I've got one more idea."

Her fingers flew over the datapad keys. Qui-Gon leaned over her shoulder to look.

"You're doing a search of the deceased register?"

"Just wait."

Qui-Gon suppressed a yawn as he stared at the screen. Finally a list of information popped up. As he scanned it, the voice recorder read it out to Tahl.

It was the same background as Tarrence Chenati. The same security clearances. The same retinal scan.

Only this Tarrence Chenati had died twenty years before.

CHAPTER 7

Obi-Wan woke at dawn. He heard the soft footsteps of the Temple students heading to meditation. He knew he should go with them. Meditation would calm his mind for the day ahead. But he could not bear to move. He did not want this day to begin.

The nighttime hours had seemed to stretch on endlessly. Obi-Wan had wanted to contact Qui-Gon, but he had nothing to say, just a longing for his Master's serene presence. He had looked for Bant, but she had told him she was going to sleep early and didn't want to talk. Just when he needed his friends, they disappeared.

Obi-Wan swung his legs over his sleep-couch. Across the room, his comlink was blinking. He hurried toward it eagerly. Maybe Qui-Gon had returned and wanted to take the morning meal together. The hearing wasn't for

hours yet. If he'd thought last night was end-
less, this morning would be even worse.

He heard Qui-Gon's voice with joy, but disappointment flooded him within seconds.

"Obi-Wan, I'm still on Centax 2. Something
has come up and I need to stay. I should be back
for the hearing."

"*Should* be?" Obi-Wan couldn't keep the anxiety out of his voice.

"You will do fine, Padawan. Speak the truth.
That is all you need."

It is not *all I need!* Obi-Wan wanted to cry. He
needed his Master's presence.

Qui-Gon sensed his dismay. "Tahl and I are
very close to solving the problems here. The
lives of Jedi pilots depend on us. I will try to
make it, Obi-Wan. Now I must go."

Qui-Gon sounded rushed. Obi-Wan said
good-bye and ended the communication. He
looked out at the spires of Coruscant, then
above to the upper atmosphere where Centax 2
was shrouded in clouds. Tahl had gone there
alone to solve the base's problems. She had
made it clear that she did not welcome Qui-
Gon's interference. Why had Qui-Gon made
the decision to support Tahl instead of his
Padawan?

Tahl had always been more important, Obi-

Wan thought bitterly. On Melida/Daan, she had been Qui-Gon's first priority. He had been anxious to get her off-planet and out of danger, even at the cost of leaving his Padawan behind. Tahl's evacuation had been more important than a civil war and a righteous cause.

He rested his hot forehead against the cool pane. He knew his thoughts were petty. He knew that his guilt about Bruck was tearing him up inside.

Bant. Bant would help him. She always had a way of seeing things clearly, yet never making him feel stupid for having the thoughts he did.

He went to her quarters, but she had already left. Obi-Wan searched for her in the meditation rooms and the dining hall, where students were beginning to gather. There was no sign of her. No one had seen her that morning.

Obi-Wan decided to go down to the Room of a Thousand Fountains. Maybe he could calm his fevered thoughts there and prepare for the ordeal ahead.

The coolness of the air hit him as he exited the turbolift. He paused to listen for the quiet rush of the hidden fountains, then moved down the overgrown paths toward the waterfall.

He threw himself on the grassy bank. The waterfall streamed over the rocks and caressed his skin with its cool, gentle spray. He gazed at the clear green of the pool, trying to calm his mind. . . .

It was like a dream. Bant was at the bottom of the pool. Her eyes were closed. Her salmon skin was pale, paler than he'd ever seen it.

This was no dream. Bant was in trouble.

Obi-Wan bounded to his feet and dived into the pool in one fluid movement. Bant's eyes opened as she saw him stroking frantically toward him. She shook her head slowly, as if to tell him to go away.

Obi-Wan ignored her. He simply scooped her up in his arms and kicked toward the surface, panic sending a burst of energy through his muscles.

He came up gasping for air. Bant sucked air in through her lungs and shook her head violently.

"No, no, let me go back —"

He dragged her to the bank and pushed her up. Bant scrambled onto the grass and collapsed. He hauled himself out and sat next to her, breathing heavily.

"What was that all about?"

Bant's face was pressed against the grass. "I was . . . testing . . . my limit," she said breathlessly.

Obi-Wan sat up. "You were *what*?"

"He said I didn't . . . know my limit," she said,

sucking in deep lungfuls of air. "If I stayed under the same amount of time and passed out, then we would know I was as close to death as I thought."

"Great plan," Obi-Wan said. "Do you mind telling me how you were going to get to the surface?"

"I rigged a chronometer to a signal that would alert security that I was in trouble," Bant said, her breathing slightly more normal. "I wasn't in danger."

"What if security didn't get here in time?" Obi-Wan demanded shakily. "What if you were already dead? You took a great risk, Bant. How could you do that to me?"

She looked up at him, astonished. "I was doing it *for* you!"

"But what if something had happened? How could you let me go through one more death?" Obi-Wan knew that the best way to convince Bant that her plan was foolish was to make her think that the greatest danger lay in hurting him.

"I didn't think of it that way," Bant said.

Obi-Wan took a deep breath to steady his voice. "Thank you for trying to help, Bant. But Qui-Gon is right. You can't. He can't. I must go through this myself. Promise me you won't do this again."

Slowly, Bant nodded. "All right. I promise," she said gravely.

"This is when we must be at our strongest," he said. "We must trust in the truth and the Force."

"And the Force will be with us," Bant said.

CHAPTER 8

"Qui-Gon was right," Tahl said to Qui-Gon and Clee Rhara. "Tarrence Chenati must have the backing of someone powerful in the Senate."

"In the Senate?" Clee asked, her eyes flashing. "A *Senator* is doing this?"

"Why not?" Qui-Gon asked mildly. "They are rarely no better and sometimes worse than most beings."

"The Senate uses its own spies," Tahl said. "They are called 'no-names.' A whole identity is created, with text docs and clearances. When the no-name dies, the identity is retired." She swept her hand toward the documents on Tarrence Chenati. "This kind of identity. What if someone had access to those retired identities and stole one for the saboteur?"

"That makes sense," Qui-Gon said. "Who would have access?"

Tahl frowned. "Hard to say. It could be almost any senior level Senator with the right contacts and the right bribes. Tracing it would be close to impossible."

"If Chenati is just a hired saboteur, he won't have much loyalty," Qui-Gon guessed. "If we capture him, he might tell us what we want to know."

"Chenati's shift starts in fifteen minutes," Clee Rhara said. "I don't want him near those ships."

"Let us handle this," Qui-Gon advised her. "Go to the students. Keep everyone away from the hangar. And try to head off Haly Dura, too."

Clee Rhara nodded. She strode off toward the student quarters. Tahl and Qui-Gon turned to go, but a signal went off on the control panel of the security system.

"It's Chenati. He's early," Qui-Gon said tersely.

Without another word, Tahl and Qui-Gon hurried to the hangar. The huge durasteel doors were already open, the starfighters lined up inside. Qui-Gon saw Chenati working on a control panel on the side of one of the starfighters.

"He's fifteen meters to the left, working on the right side of the starfighter," he said to Tahl.

"Let's flank him," she suggested. "But not until the last second. We don't want to scare him off."

Qui-Gon and Tahl strolled toward Chenati, who had caught sight of them and waved cheerfully. He reached down into his tool kit.

Something alerted Qui-Gon even before Chenati began to rise again. He was too friendly.

"He knows," Qui-Gon said.

Chenati came back up with a blaster. The fire pinged by them, since Tahl and Qui-Gon had already jumped apart. Qui-Gon's lightsaber was activated in a flash, and he sprang to deflect the blaster fire from Tahl.

"Stop protecting me!" she shouted.

But how could he? Tahl's perceptions were extraordinarily acute, but even she could not deflect rapid blaster fire she could not see. Tahl began to move in an erratic zigzag motion toward Chenati. Chenati backed away, keeping up a steady burst of fire. Qui-Gon moved forward, keeping himself between Tahl and the blaster fire. He knew she was listening for the rustle of clothing, the stir of air to tell her which way Chenati was aiming. But there was too much other noise surrounding her.

Suddenly Chenati raced into the cockpit of the starfighter. The windshield began to close.

Tahl heard the noise and began to run. The starfighter began to move, straight toward her.

"Tahl! Straight ahead!" Qui-Gon yelled. He started toward her, but Tahl had already accessed the Force and gave a great leap to her left, placing her safely out of the starfighter's way.

The distraction had cost Qui-Gon. He could not reach Chenati. He could only watch as the starship took off.

Tahl deactivated her lightsaber and tucked it into her belt in an angry motion. "Perhaps if you weren't so intent on protecting me, you could have captured him." Her voice was sharp and bitter. "Perhaps if I didn't *need* to be protected, things would be different."

"Tahl —"

"Qui-Gon! Tahl!" Clee came running up. "I saw Chenati take off." Clee stared at the sky, empty now.

"It was either kill him or let him go," Qui-Gon said.

"It's all right," Clee said. "At least we know the starfighters are safe now."

"You'll have to check these out," Tahl said. "He was here for a few minutes."

"Will do. Thank you, good friends," Clee Rhara said warmly to Qui-Gon and Tahl. She had always had a sunny nature, eager to look at the bright side of things. "We can continue the program now."

"But you don't know who your enemy is," Tahl told her.

"That worries me, it's true," Clee said. "But I'm glad to have my base back. All this suspicion was tiring."

"Yes, mistrust takes energy better spent on other things," Tahl remarked.

"Sir Tahl!" The singsong voice of Tahl's personal navigation droid, TooJay, echoed through the hangar. "You left without me this morning! Look at all the obstacles in this hangar. There is a fusioncutter by your left foot."

Tahl closed her eyes in exasperation. Usually, TooJay's fussing amused Qui-Gon. But he saw that Tahl was close to the edge now. She had had enough protection for one day.

"Tahl is fine, TooJay," he said quickly.

"Qui-Gon Jinn, hello," TooJay said. "I haven't seen you since I was reprogrammed. Lucky for me they left my memory cells intact."

Qui-Gon stopped. For a moment, he screened out his friends and the chattering droid. *He was missing something. What was it that TooJay said to trigger it?*

First Tahl and Clee talked of mistrust. Then TooJay had mentioned her reprogramming . . .

Xanatos had placed a surveillance device in TooJay. They had not known that the droid was busy transmitting their conversations to their enemy. They knew a spy was in the Temple, and Obi-Wan had suggested that Tahl could have been the one. But even though it made logical sense, Qui-Gon had never mistrusted her.

Xanatos had never been able to trust anyone. That was his downfall.

So why would he have trusted Bruck?

He remembered the feel of Bruck's lightsaber hilt, the worn quality of the carving, the small nick he had felt in the handle. It had touched him at the time, remembering the boy who had spent long hours carving it.

Everything came together then, and he knew how he could turn the tide in Obi-Wan's favor.

He hated to leave Tahl with things unsettled between them. But his Padawan needed him now.

CHAPTER 9

Obi-Wan had thought he was prepared for this. He had gone over what had happened with Bruck so many times he felt certain he could give the account smoothly. He even hoped that Vox and Kad Chun would be swayed. They would realize that the painful truth was that Bruck had chosen a dark path.

But it had not turned out that way.

From the moment he sat facing the Senators and tried to tell his story, Sano Sauro had battered him with questions. He had twisted his words. He had made him repeat himself, and if Obi-Wan made the slightest change, he pounced.

Somewhere Sano Sauro had heard that Obi-Wan and Bruck were rivals. Or perhaps he just asked the question, hoping to get an affirmative answer.

"We do not think of rivals at the Temple," Obi-Wan said. "There are certain activities that a few are especially good at. We honor that. Everyone has a special skill. Cooperation is the basis of our order."

"Isn't it true that once you fought a match that was not sanctioned by your teachers? That Bruck beat you badly and you had to hide your wounds?"

Obi-Wan looked at him, startled. How did Sano Sauro know that? The only thing he could think of was that Bruck had told Xanatos, and Xanatos had told Vox Chun. "Bruck did not beat me," he said, his eyes flashing. "The fight was a draw."

"So you say." Sano Sauro gave a chilling smile. "But you did fight."

"Bruck wanted to be Qui-Gon Jinn's Padawan. He tried to prevent me from that honor," Obi-Wan said.

Sano Sauro attacked. "So you resented him for that."

Obi-Wan had to tell the truth. "Yes," he said reluctantly. "At the time, I did."

"So Bruck Chun confessed to his Jedi leaders that he'd fought, and you tried to hide it."

Obi-Wan struggled for a moment to come up with the right answer to that question. It was true that a wounded Bruck had gone straight to the med center, but it was only to get Obi-Wan in trouble. Obi-Wan had treated his own wounds himself.

"Is that true or not?" Sano Sauro pressed.

"It is true," Obi-Wan said. "But —"

Sano Sauro twirled around and walked back to his table. "And this was the boy you say was not a rival." He threw a glance at the Senators. Senator Bicon Ransa gave a small nod.

"I did not say that, exactly," Obi-Wan said in a low tone.

"Yes, you tried very hard not to," Sano Sauro replied lightly, with another eloquent glance at the Senators. "But let us move on before we get further snared in Jedi logic. Is it true that you once left the Jedi order?"

Bant threw Obi-Wan a shocked look. Obi-Wan was just as stunned. But why should he be? Obviously Xanatos had pumped Bruck for information, gathering all he could about Qui-Gon and his Padawan. And Xanatos had told Vox.

"Yes," he said in a clear voice.

"And you were not reinstated into the Jedi order at the time of Bruck's death?"

"That is correct," Obi-Wan said.

Obi-Wan expected more questioning about his leaving the order, but Pi T'Egal interrupted.

"Is this relevant to Bruck Chun's death, Sano Sauro?" he asked sternly. "Let us proceed."

"As your honor wishes," Sano Sauro said with a slight bow.

Pi T'Egal turned to Obi-Wan. "Please tell us what happened on that day."

Obi-Wan began. Once again, he described Qui-Gon's plan to foil Xanatos. His pursuit of Bruck to the Room of a Thousand Fountains. Bruck's threat to kill Bant —

Sano Sauro interrupted. "How exactly did he threaten her life?"

"He said that Bant would die, and he didn't have to do anything. And I would have to watch it." Remembering those words, Obi-Wan felt a chill go through him almost as vivid as the one he had felt then. Bant looked down at her clasped hands.

"I see," Sano Sauro said in a tone that indicated he thought Obi-Wan was lying. "And how did you know that this was true? Did you know Bant was dying? Did you *know* that Bruck would let her die?"

"The Force was very dark in Bruck," Obi-Wan began to explain.

"Ah, the Force! I have been waiting for it to appear in testimony!" Sano Sauro declared, raising his arms. "The famous Force, which tells the Jedi what to do!"

"It does not tell us what to do," Obi-Wan said. "It binds us and connects us —"

"— and tells you that a young boy is willing to kill," Sano Sauro answered witheringly. "So therefore you kill him. Because of your mighty Force."

"The Force guided me, yes," Obi-Wan said. "But the Force never guides to kill." He threw a glance at the Senators. Jedi believed in feelings. Here at the hearing they wanted logic and facts. How could he explain that his feelings told him that Bruck had fallen so deeply into Xanatos's web of evil that he would even allow a Jedi student to die in front of his eyes?

Pi T'Egal and most of the Senators seemed to be listening intently to him without any hint that they were moved by Sano Sauro's sarcasm. But one of the Senators looked uncertain, and Bicon Ransa leaned over to whisper in her ear.

Bant looked at him, alarm in her eyes. She knew he was losing. Obi-Wan felt a sudden sweat drench his tunic. He had lost control of his testimony. Sano Sauro had twisted his words and made him look like a hotheaded fool, or worse, a dangerous liar.

"Sano Sauro, I must caution you," Pi T'Egal said. "The Jedi connection to the Force is well respected in the Senate."

Sano Sauro nodded. "I know this, Senator. Yet this Force is something that no one else can see or feel. It is something we take the Jedi's word for."

"The Jedi word is also something we respect," Senator Vi Callen said severely.

"And is this Force something that we feel confident we can judge a killing on?" Sano Sauro asked, turning to the Senators. His voice rose in intensity as he spoke. "Something only the Jedi can feel, that is used in the defense of this dangerous boy? He says he felt it. We must trust that, and exonerate him? If so, then what have our laws come to, that we mete out justice according to something that we cannot see, hear, feel, or understand? This 'Force' — what is it? What have we seen it do?"

Pi T'Egal looked to the back of the room. "Perhaps Qui-Gon Jinn can help us."

Obi-Wan looked over. Relief coursed through him at the sight of Qui-Gon standing at the back of the room, near the door.

Qui-Gon lifted a hand. Bruck's lightsaber hilt suddenly shot from the table and sailed directly into his waiting fingers.

"That is one thing the Force can do," Qui-Gon said, striding forward.

Sano Sauro paled but quickly recovered. "Tricks," he sneered.

Qui-Gon ignored him. He turned Bruck's hollow lightsaber hilt over in his hands, a look of concentration on his face. Everyone paused, watching him.

"This delay is also a stunt," Sano Sauro said, his voice turning shrill. "Let us continue . . ."

"I believe I can help put some questions to rest," Qui-Gon said quietly.

"Ah, now will we hear what the Force told *you*, Qui-Gon?" Sano Sauro asked.

"No, you will hear Bruck Chun's own words," Qui-Gon replied calmly. He turned to the Senators. "As I told you, I knew Xanatos well. He did not trust anyone, even those under his power. He would not have trusted Bruck. He would have made sure that the boy was under his complete control when he sent him back into the Temple to do his work." Qui-Gon lifted the lightsaber hilt. "He would have access to all of Bruck Chun's conversations because he would plant a listening device in the one thing that a Jedi is never without."

Obi-Wan's mouth fell open. How did Qui-Gon figure this out? He stared at the lightsaber hilt, hoping his Master was right.

Vox and Kad Chun looked at each other, startled. Sano Sauro sprang forward. "This is highly irregular! This lightsaber hilt is the property of Vox Chun!"

"This lightsaber hilt is evidence," Pi T'Egal said sternly. "You did not hesitate to employ it in your own service to gain sympathy for your client."

Qui-Gon pressed the nick in the handle and extracted a small disc. "I'll need a recorder."

The court technician took the disc and inserted it into one of the recorders on his desk.

"Let us proceed to the date and time of Bruck's death," Pi T'Egal said.

The court recorder entered the information. A moment later, Obi-Wan heard Bruck's taunting voice.

I was always better than you. Now I am even stronger.

It all came back in a rush. How he had to struggle to release his anger, how Bruck's words had seared him, how he knew Bruck was trying to anger him. . . .

Had he truly pushed his anger aside and fought with justice and calm? Sano Sauro had been right about one thing: Bruck had been his rival. There had been a deep animosity between them. He had not been able to conquer it. Even on that rocky slope.

It had been a time when he had been anxious to return to the Jedi. That longing had been a kind of fever in him. Had he told himself that he had fought without anger that day only to convince himself and Qui-Gon that he truly was a Jedi?

There was only the sound of the battle now, the ragged breath of the two of them, the slipping, sliding footwork, the buzz of the lightsabers meeting. Then Bruck's voice again, snaking out, full of venom.

She doesn't look too good, does she?

Kad Chun's shoulders jerked.

Obi-Wan heard his voice on the recorder scream Bant's name. It sounded like him but un-like him, too, the sound of someone on the edge of control, full of desperation.

Bant put her face in her hands.

And then Bruck's voice sang out, triumphant and cruel.

That's right, Obi-Wan. Bant is dying. I won't have to do a thing. I'll just make you watch it. We would have freed her if we got the treasure. But another person will die because of you. Right in front of your eyes.

Pi T'Egal made a slashing gesture at the court recorder. He switched off the machine.

"I do not think we need to subject the family to more of this," Pi T'Egal said. "The Senators will listen to the rest in private, confer, and de-liver a ruling."

A screen descended from the ceiling, obscur-ing the Senators. Obi-Wan and Qui-Gon could hear nothing. Vox and Kad Chun kept their backs to them as they conferred with Sano Sauro.

"It will be over soon," Qui-Gon said quietly.

"But how will it end?" Obi-Wan asked.

"Patience," Qui-Gon replied.

The minutes dragged by, but at last the Senators reappeared. Pi T'Egal looked at Obi-Wan, then at Vox and Kad Chun.

"The death of a young being is always tragic," he said. "The need to blame is understandable. Sometimes it is justified. But we do not think so here. We rule that Obi-Wan Kenobi is free of any responsibility in the death of Bruck Chun."

CHAPTER 10

Obi-Wan closed his eyes for an instant. Gratitude washed over him, bringing warmth to his cold skin. It felt as though his blood had been frozen and was at last able to move through his veins again.

Vox Chun spoke to Sano Sauro, but his voice was raised enough to carry throughout the room. "I should have known better than to look for justice here. Once again the Senate bows to the Jedi!"

"There is no cause for celebration or congratulation," Qui-Gon said gently to Bant and Obi-Wan. "We are glad that justice is done. But we have lost a Jedi."

Obi-Wan pressed his lips together and nodded. Now that the relief was wearing off, he realized that the guilt had not left. He had thought the verdict would remove the sense of shame he felt. But he felt no different. The burden he carried was still within him.

"Let us return to the Temple," Qui-Gon said as the Senators filed out. "Come, Obi-Wan."

"In a moment." Obi-Wan suddenly felt a need to be alone. All he had wanted the past few days was his Master and friends around him. Yet now he could not bear to be with them.

Bant started to say something, but Qui-Gon signaled her to be quiet.

"We will wait for you at the Senate entrance," he said.

Obi-Wan could only nod numbly. He had a sense of Qui-Gon and the others leaving. The table where Sano Sauro and the Chuns had sat was empty. He wondered what he felt. He did not feel much of anything.

"You must be relieved."

Kad Chun spoke behind him. Obi-Wan turned. The boy stood in the aisle, fists clenched, eyes burning.

"Sano Sauro almost got you to reveal the truth," Kad Chun went on. "You hated my brother. All your noble Jedi training failed you. You were glad to see him die."

Obi-Wan shook his head. "No . . ."

Kad shot forward unexpectedly. He swung out with his closed fist. The blow hit Obi-Wan on the side of the head near his cheekbone. He staggered back.

Kad swung again, but this time Obi-Wan was able to duck. The blow grazed his ear.

"You killed him," Kad grunted. "The one honor our family had. You killed it."

"I didn't . . ." Obi-Wan ducked again and twisted away. He tried to capture Kad Chun's arms.

With a shove that sent Obi-Wan flying back into the table, Kad Chun leaped away. He dodged behind the long table where the Senators had sat so that it was now between him and Obi-Wan.

"Kad, I didn't want your brother to die," Obi-Wan said, his breath ragged. "You heard his own words, you heard what he was willing to do!"

"He was angry! He was taunting you. So what?" Kad screamed. "It doesn't mean he would have done it!"

Obi-Wan shook his head helplessly. Kad worshiped his brother. That was clear. He could not bear to hear the truth about Bruck. He had never known him.

"He would have done it, Kad," Obi-Wan said. "I am certain of it."

"Who cares what you think!" Kad suddenly

leaped onto the Senator's table. In his hand he held the heavy wood and metal staff that Vivendi Allum had used. It was a formidable weapon. With Kad's strength, he could knock Obi-Wan out cold.

Obi-Wan knew he could neatly slice it into pieces with his lightsaber. It would only take moments. Kad was strong, but he was not trained. Obi-Wan could disarm him in a moment.

But he would not take up his lightsaber against Bruck's brother.

Kad ran toward him, his face taut with fury.

Obi-Wan watched him run at him with a strange detachment. It was as though he were in a dream. He made no move to dodge. He saw Kad's arm muscles bunch as he lifted the staff, gathering himself for the blow. Obi-Wan still did not move. He saw the staff whistle down toward his skull. . . .

At the last second, Kad twisted his wrist. The staff hit the table, splitting it in two.

Kad dropped the staff. He stared down at the floor, panting. Then he raised his gaze to Obi-Wan.

"I will never forgive you, Obi-Wan Kenobi," he rasped. "In my eyes, you will always be a killer." He kicked aside the staff and walked up the aisle toward the door.

Obi-Wan stood frozen, Kad's words echoing in his brain. *You will always be a killer.*

No matter how many meditations he had done, no matter how many talks with Qui-Gon he had had, nothing had done him any good. He could not wipe the guilt and shame from deep within himself. He knew that Kad had seen into his heart.

In his own eyes, he was a killer, too.

Twelve Years Later

CHAPTER 11

Obi-Wan moved quickly along the path that ran beside the lake. A fresh breeze moved across his skin and whispered through the branches overhead. Even after all these years, he had to remind himself that the breeze was caused by hidden cooling fans, the dappled shadow on the forest floor created by a series of illumination banks that mimicked the rise and decline of the sun.

His footsteps slowed as he heard the calls and laughter of the Jedi students at the beach along the lake. Although he had received a message that he and Anakin were to report to Yoda, he wanted a few seconds of delay. Anakin had so few opportunities for play. He hated to interrupt him.

They had been heading back from an intense physical workout when Obi-Wan had spied the students from Anakin's year heading to the lake. He had seen the longing in Anakin's eyes as the students dived into the cool water.

"Go ahead," Obi-Wan had told him. "Take some time off."

Anakin had looked at him uncertainly, but Obi-Wan shooed him off. It puzzled and worried Obi-Wan how much time his Padawan spent alone. Anakin had told him that he'd had good friends on Tatooine, especially a human boy named Kitster. He'd been at the Temple for three years now, but he hadn't made one close friend, although he was well liked and certainly got along with the other kids.

Obi-Wan had tried to talk to him about it, but the boy would just shut down. His eyes would turn opaque and the corners of his mouth would straighten into a thin line. He would seem very far away. Obi-Wan did not know how to reach him at such times, but they were infrequent and passed as quickly as a rain shower. When they'd met, Anakin had been a warm-hearted nine-year-old boy with an open nature. He was twelve and a half now, and the years had changed him. He had grown to be a boy who hid his heart.

Obi-Wan had tried to show Anakin that friends he would make at the Temple would be his for life. Obi-Wan's friends from his classes — Garen, Reeft, and Bant — were now roaming the galaxy. He didn't see them very often. But that deep tie was still there. He wanted the same for Anakin.

Qui-Gon had been dead for three and a half years. Sometimes it seemed like an age, but most of the time it seemed like it had happened yesterday. Especially when he needed his Master's advice. He would always think of Qui-Gon as his Master. Qui-Gon had been torn from him too soon, and Obi-Wan still felt his presence at his shoulder. He even knew what Qui-Gon would say right now.

You cannot make friends for your Padawan, Obi-Wan. You can only show him through your own actions how important connections are to you.

Qui-Gon had done that. Obi-Wan was still running into beings throughout the galaxy who came up to him and spoke reverently or glowingly or humorously of their deep friendship with his Master. Obi-Wan hadn't realized how many connections Qui-Gon had forged with the most unlikely sorts.

Smiling, Obi-Wan paused behind a screen of trees. He couldn't resist a moment to see if Anakin was enjoying himself with the others.

He scanned the happy, splashing group with the smile still on his face. It slowly faded as he realized that Anakin wasn't there. With a sigh, Obi-Wan turned away.

He hurried to the nearest turbolift. He knew where Anakin was. The boy sometimes retreated to his own quarters.

Obi-Wan exited at Anakin's floor and quickly made his way to the boy's quarters. As he reached them, the lower half of a protocol droid rotated out the door on its own. It was followed a moment later by a battered astromech droid, which tottered and then smashed into the wall.

Obi-Wan paused. As expected, a split second later Anakin raced out the door and crashed right into Obi-Wan.

"By the suns, I thought I had it this time," he cried, rebounding off Obi-Wan and crouching by the droid.

"I thought you wanted to swim," Obi-Wan said.

That shuttered look came over Anakin's face. "I had work to do," he muttered.

Obi-Wan crouched by him. "This isn't work, Anakin. It's a hobby. And if you are using it to keep distance between you and your fellow students, it's not a helpful one."

Anakin looked up, his bright eyes keen again.

"But I'm *making* things, Master! Look, I've almost got this astromech ready for service."

"Mechanical ability is a valuable skill," Obi-Wan said. "That is not what I meant, and you know it."

"They don't want me," Anakin said flatly. He walked over and slung the legs of the protocol droid under one arm. "I'm not like them."

Obi-Wan couldn't argue. Anakin was unique. There was no question about that. He was an exceptional student, much more in tune with the Force than others his age. He had come late to the Temple. It wasn't that the other students disliked him, they just didn't know what to make of him.

When did it happen? Obi-Wan wondered again. *Why did it happen?* Was it the loss of his mother, followed so closely by the death of Qui-Gon? Obi-Wan could not replace those people in Anakin's heart, nor did he wish to. He had hoped that with Jedi training and their own relationship, Anakin would come to find peace. He had not.

"Yoda has requested our presence," he told Anakin, rolling the astromech droid back into Anakin's quarters.

Anakin looked up, excited. "A mission?"

"I don't think so," Obi-Wan said carefully.

Barely two weeks ago, Yoda and Mace Windu had expressed doubts that Anakin was ready for a mission. Anakin lacked discipline, they said. Obi-Wan disagreed. It wasn't so much a lack of discipline that caused Anakin to break rules and send his droids scurrying over the Temple corridors. It was partially boredom, he thought. No matter what he threw at Anakin, the boy mastered it. He needed more challenges. Where Yoda and Mace Windu saw a lack of discipline, Obi-Wan saw an emotional restlessness that could not be cured by hard study or physical trials.

"Straighten your tunic," he admonished. "And wash the grease off your hands."

Anakin scurried to comply, running to the sink in the corner. His quarters were crammed with tools and droid parts. Pieces of a probe droid were scattered over his sleep-couch. A pair of legs for a bipedal droid sat in a corner. Obi-Wan knew that Anakin had found these things by sneaking out of the Temple and dealing in the thriving black market of Coruscant. He preferred to turn a blind eye. So far, Yoda and Mace Windu did as well. But it did not help Anakin's reputation with the Council.

Anakin cleaned up and hurried to keep step with Obi-Wan. Obi-Wan could tell that he was bursting with questions, but uncharacteristically, he did not ask them. Obi-Wan could not have answered them if he had.

Yoda awaited them in a meditation room, the place he favored now for conferences. Obi-Wan knew that Yoda had often met Qui-Gon at his favorite bench in the Room of a Thousand Fountains. Yoda never sat there now. It was the only visible sign that Yoda still was in deep mourning for his friend.

"A request the Council has for you both," Yoda announced without preliminaries.

Anakin could not contain his excitement. "A mission?"

Yoda blinked his gray-blue eyes and did not answer. He studied Anakin for a moment. Obi-Wan was often charmed by Anakin's enthusiasm, but it seemed to worry Yoda.

"A mission it is not," Yoda said. "But a voyage you must take. Request we do that you travel to a starship called the *BioCruiser,* a permanent home for a group of people gathered from many worlds in the galaxy. Those on the ship have come from damaged worlds — planets that have become toxic or ravaged by disease or torn apart by criminal gangs or civil war. Land on other worlds they do not. Roam the galaxy they do."

"You mean they live on board a ship?" Anakin's gaze grew wider. "Lucky."

"How do they manage it?" Obi-Wan asked. "What about food and supplies?"

"Grow their own food they do," Yoda answered. "Self-sustaining, they are. But stop they must for fuel and for occasional supplies. Meet them you will at the next docking point. Complaints the Senate has received from the families of those aboard." Yoda drew his robes around him. "Fear they do that their loved ones have been coerced or brainwashed."

"Who leads this group?" Obi-Wan asked.

"Uni is the name he goes by," Yoda answered. "No text doc information can we find about him. Agreed Uni has to a Jedi inspection to calm the worries of the Senate. Danger for you we do not anticipate. Only a few days should this require."

Obi-Wan nodded and kept his skepticism to himself. He had heard these words before, and had been plunged into danger and disarray.

"So we are to travel far away to a ship where people might be held hostage," Anakin said shrewdly. "It sure sounds like a mission to me."

"A request only," Yoda corrected.

Telling them that he would provide further details of the rendezvous soon, Yoda dismissed them. Anakin was silent as they left.

As soon as they rounded the corner, he

turned to Obi-Wan, a delighted grin on his face. "My first mission!"

"Request," Obi-Wan said sternly. But he saw Anakin shake his head and silently mouth the word "mission" with a smile.

CHAPTER 12

The next scheduled fuel stop for the *Bio-Cruiser* was on the planet Hilo. Yoda arranged for a transport to pick up Obi-Wan and Anakin at the landing platform.

Obi-Wan stood, looking up last-minute information about Hilo on his datapad. Anakin's gaze remained fixed on the skies of Coruscant; every so often he exclaimed about a ship that zoomed by in the crowded space lanes.

"Master, look at that starship!" he called suddenly. "Have you ever seen such a beauty?"

Obi-Wan looked up. A sleek starship was negotiating the tight traffic lanes, jockeying for position. "A diplomat or Senator's transport, most likely," he said, noting the chromium trim on the sleek black ship.

He watched as the skillful pilot found space to slide into the teeming lane, then made a sharp turn to come toward them. To Obi-Wan's surprise, the beautiful ship landed on the Jedi platform.

"Maybe that's our transport!" Anakin cried.

The ramp lowered and a familiar figure strode down toward them.

"Garen!" Obi-Wan was overjoyed to see his friend. It had been several years since Garen had been to the Temple.

He hurried toward him, and the two friends clapped their arms around each other in a fierce hug.

"This is a surprise," Obi-Wan said, quickly taking in his friend's appearance. He was relieved to see that Garen looked as fit and healthy as ever. His hair was still worn long and loose, waving past his collar, and his gaze was as open and warm as Obi-Wan remembered. He knew that Garen had been on a difficult mission in the Outer Rim, though he didn't know the details.

"You look older," Garen said. "But wiser? I'll have to hope for that." His eyes danced.

Obi-Wan grinned. "You haven't changed at all."

"I was sorry to hear about Qui-Gon," Garen said, his mood abruptly changing. "I would have come, but . . ."

"It is all right, my friend. It was a great loss for the Jedi."

"And for you."

"Yes. He was my friend as well as my Master," Obi-Wan said. He did not speak of Qui-Gon to many people. He still found it too painful, even after all this time. "But let me introduce you to my Padawan."

"How strange it is to hear you say that," Garen said, smiling. "Now we are old enough to have our own Padawans. Who would have thought it?"

Anakin had been hanging back, studying the ship with avid eyes. When he saw Obi-Wan's welcoming glance, he hurried forward.

"Is this your ship?"

"Anakin," Obi-Wan said reprovingly. "This is my good friend, Jedi Knight Garen Muln. Garon, this is Anakin Skywalker."

"I am honored to meet you at last," Garen said. "No, this isn't my ship. It's a royal starship from the Bimin Three system, on extended loan for the Jedi."

"I knew you'd end up with a starship somehow," Obi-Wan said.

Garen nodded ruefully. Obi-Wan knew he had been bitterly disappointed when the Jedi decided to end the starfighter program. But Garen had gone on to become Clee Rhara's Padawan and had distinguished himself on missions throughout the galaxy.

"It turned out for the best," Garen said. "I think in the end the Council was right to oppose the starfighter pilot program. A fleet of starfighters would have brought us trouble."

"Do you mean the Jedi once had a program for starfighter pilots?" Anakin asked, stunned at this news.

"Yes, Anakin, long ages ago, back when Obi-Wan and I were only a little older than you," Garen said, laughing.

"And they *cancelled* it?" Anakin's face showed clearly what he thought of that decision.

"It was for the best," Garen said. "But I must admit it was fun while it lasted."

Anakin gazed at the ship. "How fast does she go?"

"As fast as you want," Garen answered. He looked at Anakin curiously. "Why do you like to go fast, Anakin?"

The dreamy, shuttered look came over Anakin's face. "Because I can leave myself behind," he said, his eyes on the ship.

Garen glanced at Obi-Wan. He raised one eyebrow. It was not a Jedi answer. Obi-Wan frowned, troubled by it. There were still places in Anakin he could not reach.

No. You will reach them. Yoda and Mace

Windu are wrong. Qui-Gon was right. Anakin is not too old to learn.

Garen put his hand on Anakin's shoulder. "Let me show you the ship."

"We're waiting for our transport to Hilo," Anakin said, disappointed. "I don't think my Master will allow it."

"Oh, I think he will," Garen said. "*I'm* your transport to Hilo."

Anakin seemed stunned at his good fortune. A delighted grin lit up his face, and he ran ahead to race up the ramp.

Garen picked up Obi-Wan's survival pack. "He seems very young," he observed.

Obi-Wan sighed. "He is getting older every day."

They came out of hyperspace to a rush of stars. It was Anakin's favorite moment, Obi-Wan knew. He watched the boy's face, alert with interest as Garen piloted the ship toward the atmosphere of Hilo.

Garen whistled. "There she is."

The largest ship Obi-Wan had ever seen rose ahead of them. It seemed to be many ships welded together, made up of different metals and rivets and fasteners, so that dull green gave way to flashing silver to gleaming black.

It chugged in a slow, lazy orbit around the planet.

"We're supposed to land on Hilo to pick up a transport back to the ship," Garen said. "Apparently they don't allow outsiders to dock on the ship."

"I've never seen anything like that," Anakin said. He got up from his seat to stand close to the cockpit viewport. He grinned and shot a mischievous look back at Obi-Wan. "It looks like something I might have built."

Obi-Wan had to agree. It had the chunky, cobbled-together look of some of Anakin's practice constructions.

The landing platform loomed ahead, a light freighter parked to one side. As they drew closer, Obi-Wan could see that supplies were being loaded.

Garen made his usual perfect landing. He helped Anakin and Obi-Wan gather their packs and walked them down the ramp.

Obi-Wan and Garen exchanged a look of friendship and farewell, one they had exchanged many times over the years.

"May the Force be with you," Garen said. "I can transport you back if you need me. I'll be in this quadrant for a bit."

"May the Force be with you," Obi-Wan told him.

Garen turned and strode up the ramp. He did not turn for a final good-bye. He never did. Only Obi-Wan knew that his old friend hated farewells.

"You are the Jedi inspection team." The tone was curt and businesslike. Obi-Wan turned to see a tall, balding human in a unigarment of pale blue.

"I am Obi-Wan Kenobi and this is Anakin Skywalker," Obi-Wan answered.

"I am Nort Fandi," the man said. "I am the freighter pilot. We are scheduled to depart. Board the craft. We do not linger on other worlds."

There was no trace of friendliness or courtesy in Nort Fandi's curt tone. Obi-Wan and Anakin boarded the freighter and found seats. In just a few minutes, Nort Fandi and two crew members joined them. Within seconds, they blasted off toward the *BioCruiser*.

"Will you be taking us directly to Uni?" Obi-Wan asked Nort Fandi.

He did not turn. "No. You will be given instructions."

He did not say another word. As they approached the *BioCruiser*, hatch doors slid open in the main ship and Obi-Wan saw the landing area. Nort Fandi slid the freighter inside. The engines powered down.

A short woman in the same pale blue unigarment stood waiting as they walked down the ramp.

"I am Deleta," she said. "I am to show you to your cabins."

"Will we meet with Uni after that?" Obi-Wan asked.

Deleta led them to a bank of turbolifts. "He will contact you shortly."

Obi-Wan picked up no fear or anxiety in the many beings they passed on the way to their sleeping quarters. There were beings from across the galaxy, some wearing the same pale blue garments, some in tunics, some sporting a headdress or leggings from their home worlds. They appeared busy and calm, and he could discern no evidence of thought control. Their gazes were clear and focused as they regarded Obi-Wan and Anakin with lively curiosity.

The Jedi's quarters were small and spare, but with a shared small library, a cubicle for showering, and even a small cooler with fresh juices and snacks.

"Meals will be brought to you," Deleta said. "Do not wander the ship alone. If you wish a tour, one will be arranged for you shortly."

"How can I contact Uni?" Obi-Wan asked.

"He will contact you shortly," Deleta answered serenely, and left.

* * *

"So what do you think 'shortly' means here on the cruiser?" Anakin grumbled. He lay back on his sleep-couch on his elbows, his expression sulky. "A year? More?"

"It's been two days," Obi-Wan said. "Each mission takes its own time." He repeated the words automatically. Like Anakin, he, too, felt frustrated. Any additional requests he had made to speak to Uni or even to get a tour of the ship had met with the same "You will be contacted shortly." When he and Anakin had ventured out on their own, they had been politely and firmly escorted back to their quarters and told they would be contacted . . . "shortly."

At first Obi-Wan had been reluctant to press the issue. They were guests of the *BioCruiser*, and he never liked to start out a mission by being insistent. But he had his limits, and he had reached them.

Obi-Wan pressed the button on the built-in message console. As always, he was addressed by a pleasant, neutral voice.

"May I be of service?"

"I would like to leave a message for Uni," Obi-Wan said.

"He will contact you shortly —"

"Fine. Please inform him that if he does not meet with us in ten minutes I will call back my transport and the full power of the Senate will be unleashed against the *BioCruiser*."

Obi-Wan did not wait for a reply but cut off the connection.

Anakin was now sitting erect. "Will you really do that?"

"Jedi do not threaten," Obi-Wan said. "We inform." He sat calmly, but his eyes were on the chrono. Anything could happen. They could be locked inside their quarters. Or Uni could decide to boot them off the ship to the nearest planet.

In exactly eight minutes, the door hissed open. Deleta stood with the same neutral expression on her face.

"Uni will see you now."

Obi-Wan and Anakin followed her through a maze of corridors to a single turbolift. It brought them to a higher level of the ship. They emerged into a deserted hallway.

Deleta accessed a door at the far end of the corridor. They walked into a round room lined with low seating and recessed glow lights. The walls, floors, and furniture were pale blue. Deleta left, the doors hissing shut behind her.

"Do you think this is Uni's private quarters?" Anakin asked in a hushed tone.

"Most likely," Obi-Wan answered.

The doors opened behind him. Obi-Wan saw

a tall, slender human walk in. His hair was close-cropped and as white as a moon. His eyes were clear and very blue.

"I am Uni," he said.

But Obi-Wan knew immediately that it was Kad Chun.

CHAPTER 13

Obi-Wan felt as if his throat had been squeezed. His feet were planted on the floor, or else he could have sworn that he staggered.

"Kad Chun." Obi Wan spoke his name numbly.

Kad looked just as surprised. He gathered himself with a visible effort. "Obi-Wan Kenobi. I am Uni now."

Kad approached until he was standing close to Obi-Wan, closer than Obi-Wan liked. His pale eyes flickered as he registered the signs of maturity in Obi-Wan. Obi-Wan remembered the face of the boy, burning with hatred in a Senate hearing room.

"So they sent you."

"Yes."

"I suppose they do not know who I am."

"No."

"Kad Chun is no more."

Obi-Wan's curiosity overcame his caution. "How did you come to be here?"

Kad turned and began to stroll about the room. He did not give Anakin a glance, but the boy watched him steadily.

"After the hearing, my father and I returned to Telos. We led a quiet life, recovering from our double tragedy — the loss of our son and brother, and the inability of the Senate to bring his killer to justice."

Obi-Wan stiffened, but Uni did not look at him, just strolled about, picking up an object here or there, studying it and putting it down.

"Many good things happened on Telos. I understand you were there at the beginning. A new government was formed, and the reclamation of our natural resources began. But as the years passed it became clear that the corruption that had destroyed our institutions and government had taken a deeper hold than the good people of Telos imagined. Special interests again took over. Telos began a steep decline. Corporations owned our natural resources and plundered them."

"I am sorry to hear this," Obi-Wan said.

"I found myself in a position of some leadership," Kad went on. "I gathered followers. I knew it was too late to save Telos. We were wasting our time. We could never fight that kind of power. In order to save the remaining examples of responsibility and honor on Telos, we had to bring the last of the best with us. Which we did. We boarded a ship, taking our plants and minerals with us. We traveled through the galaxy. We did not look for another world. We did not need one. As we traveled I saw that Telos was not unique. So many worlds in the galaxy are corrupt. The noblest beings protest and are drowned out. We welcomed them aboard. Our core ship began to grow. We have the most brilliant scientists, the greatest innovators, teachers, poets, musicians, doctors. We all believe that given the state of the galaxy the only choice for the best of us is to disengage from it completely. After the galaxy destroys itself we will be the seed for a new community."

Kad turned at last. His pale blue eyes burned with fervor. "So you see no one here is held against their will. They can leave at any time at our next docking port. We are working on a renewable fuel that we can produce on the ship, but we haven't been able to perfect it. So we must still stop occasionally. We hope one day to be completely self-sufficient. We will not ever need to have contact with another world. Until then we must deal with the tiresome demands of the Senate. I consider it demeaning to the intelligence of all who live aboard this ship. Nevertheless, I will cooperate."

"You will allow us access throughout the ship?"

Kad nodded. "I will arrange a tour so you can get an overview. After that, you are free to wander on your own."

"We can speak to any of your followers?"

Kad frowned. "I do not use the word *followers.*"

"These beings are here because of your philosophy?"

"A philosophy they have adopted as their own." Kad raised an eyebrow. "And what about the Jedi? How different are we from you? Yet the Senate does not send envoys to investigate you, I notice."

"We are very different. We lead lives of contemplation but also engagement," Obi-Wan said in the even tone he adopted when he was irritated. "We do not isolate ourselves and abandon the galaxy."

"Yes, you still believe you can do good," Kad said carelessly. "Everyone on this ship felt that way once."

Obi-Wan sensed that disengaging was a good philosophy to adopt at that moment. He knew it was fruitless to argue with Kad and knew that Kad's carelessness was studied. He was goading Obi-Wan. No doubt he knew that Obi-Wan's calm was also a mask.

"I am sorry you consider this process demeaning," Obi-Wan said carefully. "But I'm sure you must realize that there are family members throughout the galaxy who have to deal with the sudden disappearance of their loved ones. Communication has been infrequent."

"That is because no one understands our vision," Kad said impatiently. "Everyone here is an adult, capable of making their own decisions. Now, I suggest that you and your *follower* proceed to the bridge, where I have arranged for one of us to give you a tour of the ship. Take the turbolift to Level four and you will be met there."

The doors opened again. A frail old man walked slowly into the room. His scalp gleamed in the light, and his hooded eyes were dull. It took Obi-Wan several seconds to remember Vox Chun. He was startled at how much he had aged.

Vox Chun's dull gaze suddenly blazed into rage. It was obvious that his hatred of Obi-Wan had not diminished with the years.

"Father, the Jedi team is proceeding to the bridge for a tour," Kad said quickly. Obi-Wan saw that he wanted to forestall any outburst.

Obi-Wan nodded at Vox Chun, who did not return the greeting. He kept his burning gaze on Obi-Wan as he and Anakin crossed the room and walked out the doors.

The doors shut behind them. Anakin looked up at him.

"Why do they hate you?"

"Old history," Obi-Wan said. "Missions can leave grievances behind. I do not think it will affect the present."

Anakin nodded, but Obi-Wan could tell he was not satisfied; he believed that old grievances *would* affect this mission.

The trouble was, so did Obi-Wan. It was not the first time that Obi-Wan found it inconvenient to have such an astute Padawan.

CHAPTER 14

Anakin trudged alongside Obi-Wan, wondering about the title of Padawan Learner. That implied that he was supposed to learn, didn't it? How could he learn when he never had the full story?

Yoda was full of riddles. Mace Windu spoke in hints and allusions. Even his Master deflected most talk of the past, except for affectionate or respectful references to his old Master. Sometimes it seemed to Anakin that everyone at the Temple spoke a different language from the one he knew. It was at such times that he missed his mother's warm clarity. But remembering Shmi brought back an ache so deep it never went away.

"At least we'll get a tour of the ship," Obi-Wan remarked as they waited for the turbolift. "You've been wanting to explore it."

"But we'll have a guide," Anakin said. "They probably won't show us the whole thing. Wouldn't you rather explore on your own?"

"Sometimes it is helpful to see what your opponent wishes you to see," Obi-Wan said, stepping into the turbolift. "It can indicate what he is trying to hide."

Anakin stood quietly as the levels ticked off. He was still out of sorts from first being ignored in the meeting between Obi-Wan and Uni, and then not being told the truth by Obi-Wan. He had felt the dark anger from both Vox and Uni, the man Obi-Wan called Kad. Those two held more than a simple grievance against his Master. Why didn't Obi-Wan trust him enough to tell him the truth?

The turbolift doors opened and Anakin got another surprise. Obi-Wan broke into a broad smile at the sight of a slender woman standing waiting for them.

"Is it Andra?" he asked.

The woman looked just as surprised and pleased. "Obi-Wan Kenobi!"

Obi-Wan and the woman stepped forward. Andra grasped Obi-Wan's hand. "I have never forgotten you."

"What a surprise to see you here," Obi-Wan said. "I imagined you would be ruler of Telos by now."

Andra's face darkened. "The Telos I fought for is gone. My life is here now."

"Yes, Kad told me how it deteriorated."

"We call him Uni now. Yes, we defeated Offworld, but other equally powerful concerns took over. I watched my beautiful planet deteriorate for the second time. I could do nothing. My rage and frustration turned to deep sorrow. It was as though I was in a dark place with no way out. Then I met Uni." Andra shook her head as if to dislodge dark memories. "Uni gave me a reason to live." She looked over at Anakin and smiled. "And who is this?"

"This is my Padawan, Anakin Skywalker."

Andra gave him a warm nod of greeting. Anakin liked her immediately. He felt a kind of warmth and acceptance from her that reminded him of Shmi.

"So you have your own Padawan now," she said, the smile still on her face as she glanced at Obi-Wan. "Qui-Gon must miss you."

Obi-Wan's bright gaze dimmed. "Andra, Qui-Gon is dead. Three years now."

Her smile vanished, and sorrow filled her eyes. "I did not know. I am so sorry. The galaxy is diminished without him."

"Yes," Obi-Wan said. "That is exactly how I feel. But what about Den? Still getting on your nerves?"

"I'm afraid so," Andra said ruefully. "I married him."

Obi-Wan laughed. Den and Andra were an odd match, but Qui-Gon had seen how much deep love there was between them. "Is he aboard the *BioCruiser* as well?"

"Of course. He was resistant at first. But he came to see the truth of Uni's teachings." Andra paused. "You must be the Jedi come to inspect us. I am to give you the tour."

"I can ask for no better guide," Obi-Wan said.

Anakin hurried forward as Andra turned to walk down the corridor with them. "How do you two know each other?" he asked her. Better to ask Andra than Obi-Wan. He'd get a more complete story.

"Obi-Wan and Qui-Gon helped our world when it was dying," Andra explained. "A mining corporation called Offworld had secretly bought up our national park spaces and had begun to mine them. I was part of the underground then —"

"A one-woman underground," Obi-Wan said admiringly.

"True, I didn't have many followers at the time," Andra said ruefully. "Just a thief and gambler short on ethics and long on charm. He became my husband, Den. Despite the fact that we were outlaws, Obi-Wan and Qui-Gon trusted us. They exposed Offworld, and the people got control of our sacred spaces again. Or so we thought. In the end, we lost the battle."

Andra stopped in the middle of the circular bridge. "But I'll never forget what they did for us."

"And what *you* did for *us*," Obi-Wan pointed out. "You saved us from execution."

"Execution?" Anakin asked, staring at Obi-Wan, wide-eyed.

"Xanatos was a terrible enemy," Andra said softly.

"Xanatos?" Anakin asked.

"A story for another time," Obi-Wan said firmly.

Andra nodded, understanding that Obi-Wan wished to change the subject. She gestured at the busy workers surrounding them and the banks of controls. "As you can see, our bridge is more complicated than most starships'. The *BioCruiser* is made of different components, some of them originally designed to run differently from others'. Here is where everything is coordinated. Already our scientists have discovered a number of technological breakthroughs. The size and complexity of the ship is unprecedented."

"Do you have a defense system?" Obi-Wan asked.

Andra nodded. "State of the art. We have a valuable treasury aboard. Each of us brought all our assets aboard when we joined. We use that money for research and development. Eventually, we want to be a fully self-sustaining ship, as though we were a floating planet."

"Most planets are not fully self-sustaining," Obi-Wan pointed out. "They depend on trade and the free exchange of information."

"When you open your doors to the galaxy, you invite corruption to overtake you," Andra said, shaking her head. "I have seen it happen on Telos. I have talked to many aboard who have seen it happen on their own worlds. Criminal gangs grow more powerful every day in the galaxy. More and more, giant corporations gobble up natural resources. They just move on to the next planet ripe for exploitation. I believe that Uni is right. This," Andra concluded, spreading her arms to take in the ship, "is our greatest hope. Now, let us proceed. We have much to see."

Anakin had never seen such a fascinating ship. It was crowded with beings from all over the galaxy, and there seemed to be plenty to do. Most of the beings worked at least part of the day, either in the tech centers, scientific labs, or service industries. There were all kinds of restaurants and cafés, with food from many worlds. There were game rooms and libraries and music rooms. One whole area of the *BioCruiser* was devoted to the Collection Center, where plants, flowers, and animals from many worlds were kept. Anakin could not imagine ever being bored. He wasn't sure how he felt about Uni's philosophy, but he thought living aboard a ship would be outstanding.

The tour took several hours. Andra left them at their quarters.

"I hope you can tell the Senate that we wish no harm. All aboard are here of their free will," she said to Obi-Wan.

"I hope so as well," Obi-Wan answered politely.

Andra cocked her head. "Ah. I had forgotten how noncommittal the Jedi can be."

"We reserve our judgment until we can speak plainly," Obi-Wan said. "We enjoyed the tour, Andra. Thank you."

"I'll tell Den you're aboard. I'm sure he'd like to see you." With a last friendly wave, Andra headed off.

As soon as she was gone, Anakin turned to Obi-Wan. "Who is Xanatos?"

The question seemed to startle Obi-Wan. But Anakin had sensed something when Andra had mentioned the name. He had felt something from Obi-Wan, something he wanted to know more about.

"Not now," Obi-Wan said.

"Shortly?" Anakin asked, discouraged. "I keep hearing that word. Why won't you tell me now? Is there some reason I can't know?" Again, he felt frustrated. It was hard to penetrate Obi-Wan's reserve.

Obi-Wan studied him for a moment. "No," he said finally. "There is no reason you can't know. Xanatos was a former apprentice of Qui-Gon's. He turned to the dark side. He used the Force to build his own power. He was the head of the Offworld Mining Corporation and laid waste to whole worlds. Life meant nothing to him."

"Is he still alive?" Anakin asked.

"He died on Telos," Obi-Wan answered. "He preferred to take his own life rather than surrender to Qui-Gon." He studied Anakin for a moment. "Now let's clean up and go out for the evening meal."

Anakin went into his quarters. He felt a buzzing in his head, as if his thoughts were so numerous and confused that they could not register. He could not take in what Obi-Wan had told him. He could not imagine that such a thing could happen. How could a Jedi turn to the dark side? How could a Padawan betray his Master?

If he hadn't heard the story from Obi-Wan, he would have refused to believe it.

At last Obi-Wan had shared something real with him. There were times, especially early on, when Anakin questioned Obi-Wan's motive in taking him on as Padawan. He knew Obi-Wan had done it because it was Qui-Gon's wish. Was he a burden to Obi-Wan? Just a promise made to a dying friend? More than anything, Anakin longed to have the kind of bond with Obi-Wan that his Master had had with Qui-Gon. There were times when that closeness seemed very far away.

CHAPTER 15

Alone in his cabin, Obi-Wan splashed cold water on his face. When he raised his head and gazed into the small mirror over the sink, he was almost surprised to see his mature face. He had been plunged back into his boyhood twice today. It left him feeling rocked and tentative, as though he was once again that thirteen-year-old boy.

Seeing Andra was a pleasure. It brought back a satisfying memory. The mission on Telos had been treacherous, but Obi-Wan remembered it as a time when he and Qui-Gon had begun to rebuild the bonds between them after he had left the Jedi and his Master for a short time. They had worked together in the old rhythm, and for the first time since Obi-Wan had left, Qui-Gon had truly welcomed him back. He had made Obi-Wan feel that their bond was strong and would grow even stronger. As it did.

But Kad . . . *Uni,* Obi-Wan corrected himself.

That confrontation had been less pleasant. He still remembered the hate in Kad's eyes, the sound of the table splintering as the rod came down, the knowledge that this boy wanted to kill him. And how he had waited for the blow, defenseless, feeling that in some way if the blow fell he would at last be at peace with Bruck's death. He would have paid a debt.

He had never told Qui-Gon about that moment. It was not the way a Jedi should think, or feel. He should have felt peace with the outcome of his battle with Bruck.

But, Obi-Wan thought, staring bleakly at his mature reflection, twelve years later he still had no peace.

He wrenched his mind back to the present. He had noted his Padawan's admiration of the workings of the *BioCruiser*. There was much to admire. But Obi-Wan was disturbed by Uni's philosophy. To his mind, the *BioCruiser* held a gathering of disillusioned idealists. Uni's philosophy of withdrawal was based in anger and bitter disappointment.

He did not like the change in Andra. He remembered her as a fierce defender of her planet. Had Uni caught her in such a low time in her life that he had tapped into her bitterness and sense of futility?

Obi-Wan had been on missions that had

seemed hopeless at the start. He had seen criminals win, of course. He had seen civil war tear worlds apart. But he had also seen beings band together to fight for their planet and succeed against impossible odds. Uni's philosophy did not impress him. Uni was a cynic hiding behind a veil of idealism.

He was also disturbed by the idea that all who joined the *BioCruiser* donated their wealth to the treasury. Andra had said this offhandedly, but Obi-Wan had to wonder who controlled such vast sums and who had access to them. Kad? His father? He still did not trust Vox Chun. Despite his supposed rehabilitation, Obi-Wan did not forget his part in the plundering of Telos. He was surprised that Andra could. She seemed to have left her healthy skepticism back on her home planet.

Still deep in thought, Obi-Wan fetched Anakin and suggested the nearby café for the evening meal. He would like a chance to observe the inhabitants of the *BioCruiser* when they were relaxed and at ease.

Anakin was soon engrossed in his food, which was fresh and delicious. Food meant less to Obi-Wan as he grew older. He had come to realize what a good Master Qui-Gon had been, in small ways as well as large ones. Qui-Gon had treated him as a Jedi, but never forgot he was a growing boy. If he hadn't had Qui-Gon's example, Obi-Wan wondered if he'd be as sensitive to Anakin's needs as he tried to be.

Obi-Wan ate methodically. He glanced casually around the crowded room, but he was alert and attuned to every gesture. He watched carefully how the various diners interacted with one another.

Suddenly a tall man plopped down in a chair opposite him, a wide grin creasing his rugged face. "So. What are the odds?"

Obi-Wan grinned back. "Den!"

"It's good to see you again, my friend. If someone told me you'd end up on this rust-bucket, I never would have taken the bet." Den grinned amiably at Anakin. "Hey there, kid. I heard you like big ships."

"I like most ships," Anakin said, his mouth full.

"Not me. I prefer to have my feet on the ground."

"So what are you doing here?" Obi-Wan asked, pushing his empty plate away. Den looked only a little older than he had all those years before. His sandy hair was still boyishly tousled, and the smile lines around his eyes were only a little deeper.

Den's pleasant expression did not falter. "Escaping the horrors of corruption and environmental degradation. What about you?"

"Investigating you," Obi-Wan shot bac. had forgotten the bumpy rhythms of Den's speech, the way he seemed to treat no subject seriously. He remembered how Qui-Gon had accepted Den immediately and had been amused by him. It had taken Obi-Wan a bit longer to get used to the fact that they were depending on a thief to help them on an important mission.

"Yes, Andra told me," Den said. "Why don't I walk you back to your quarters?"

Obi-Wan nodded. Anakin combined the three remaining bites on his plate into one and hurriedly crammed it into his mouth. Still chewing, he followed Obi-Wan and Den from the café.

"Tell me how you truly feel," Obi-Wan said quietly to Den as they strolled down the corridor.

Den sighed. "I only joined up because I didn't want to lose Andra."

"Ah," Obi-Wan said. Den had confirmed what he'd suspected. He couldn't imagine independent Den surrendering to someone else's idea of how to live.

"The ironic thing is, I was the one to make her go to Uni's lecture," Den went on. "She was in a bad state, Obi-Wan. You have to understand that many felt the same. Telos was dying, and no one could save it. Uni offered hope. Andra was first organizers of the *BioCruiser*." ...ade a wry face. "She had a cause again."

"You tried to talk her out of going?"

"Sure. I told her we should stay and fight for Telos. Or emigrate to another world, not reject the galaxy and become crazy nomads. Naturally she agreed to everything I said. Joke! Since when does Andra ever agree with me?" Den asked morosely. "I had no choice. I pretended to swallow this wacky idea, and I came aboard. Something didn't smell right to me, and it still doesn't. Listen, I may have gone straight for Andra's sake, but the criminal antennae never die. There's something wrong with this operation."

"Tell me," Obi-Wan urged.

Den waved cheerfully at a group across the corridor. "Things just don't feel right. I'm not sure about Uni, but Vox definitely has my antennae quivering. He managed to convince everyone on Telos that he had nothing to do with handing our sacred spaces over to Offworld, even though he was in Xanatos's pocket. He keeps to himself on the *BioCruiser*, stays up in those fancy quarters of his. But twice I've spotted him having a pretty intense conversation with a tech worker named Kern."

"Why is that suspicious?" Obi-Wan asked.

"Vox thinks he's too good for the rest of us,"

Den said, his eyes narrowing. "Why would he waste his time talking to some low-level tech worker?" Den tapped his nose. "I'm telling you. Doesn't smell right."

"Anything else?" Obi-Wan asked.

"Whenever we dock for fuel and supplies, it's always at some industrial planet," Den said. "Why is that? And why is Vox always among the landing party?"

"He wasn't back at Hilo," Obi-Wan pointed out.

"Yeah. I noticed that. I figure he didn't want to ride back with the Jedi team. Maybe he thought it would be suspicious if he went down. Who knows?" Den tapped his nose again and wrinkled his face as if he'd smelled something foul.

They stopped in front of their quarters. Anakin's eyes were on Den. Obi-Wan could see the boy was listening intently.

"I don't know, Den," Obi-Wan said. "You don't have much for us to go on."

"Did you know that one of the reasons we stopped at Hilo was to do a repair that didn't need to be done?" Den asked. "It turned out to be a readout malfunction. The actual part was fine."

"That happens —"

"— sometimes, I know. But guess who's in charge of readout systems? Kern."

Obi-Wan nodded, but he still wasn't convinced. He sensed that Den was searching for anything that would prove that the *BioCruiser* operation was corrupt. His desire to have his wife back could be coloring his perceptions.

"Now that you're here, my odds of getting to the bottom of this just improved a thousand percent," Den said, slapping Obi-Wan on the back. "Get a good night's sleep. You'll need it."

Den gave them a cheerful wave and hurried off. Obi-Wan sighed.

"You don't trust him?" Anakin asked.

"It's not that," Obi-Wan said. "I'm just not sure I trust his perceptions."

"But he's thinking like a Jedi," Anakin pointed out. "He's trusting his feelings. Shouldn't we honor that? Besides, we don't have any other paths to follow at the moment."

Sometimes, Anakin reminded Obi-Wan of Qui-Gon. He had the same mix of logic and emotion that Obi-Wan struggled so hard to balance.

"I trust my *own* feelings," Obi-Wan finally muttered. "Not Den's."

CHAPTER 16

Obi-Wan and Anakin had barely finished their morning meal when Den came to Obi-Wan's quarters.

"I have a way to break into the text-doc files on the *BioCruiser*," Den announced.

"I thought you had given up being a criminal," Obi-Wan said.

Den shrugged. "I was bored. It's been a long time since I got a chance to flex my muscles." His eyes twinkled. "Don't you want to see Kern's background?"

"If the Senate finds out that the Jedi illegally broke into the *BioCruiser*'s confidential records, it could compromise the investigation," Obi-Wan said with a frown. "I don't think —"

Den flourished a sheaf of durasheets. "Too late! I printed out the information for you."

"Great!" Anakin enthused. "Now we can start."

Den grinned. "I like your style, kid."

With a sigh, Obi-Wan took the durasheets. He quickly glanced through the information, absorbing it. Then he handed it to Anakin.

"You see the problem?" Den asked Obi-Wan. He nodded.

"I don't get it," Anakin said. "Everything seems in order to me. He's got top-level security clearance. From the Senate, even. Isn't that hard to get?"

"Yes," Obi-Wan said. "*Very* hard. That's why there's a problem."

"Why would a low-level tech worker like Kern need high-security clearance from the Senate?" Den asked.

"It's odd, but it doesn't necessarily have significance," Obi-Wan said. "It probably just means that he worked on sensitive material at one point. Everyone has a past."

Den collapsed in a nearby chair. "If you're going to think that everything I bring you is useless, we're not going to get anywhere."

"Relax, Den. I didn't say we wouldn't follow up." Motioning to Anakin, Obi-Wan stood. "As a matter of fact, I'd like a more complete tour this morning. Do you think you can lead us to the tech center?"

Den indicated Kern with a nod as they entered the tech center. He was a good ten years older than Obi-Wan, with close-cropped light hair and eyes set close together.

"This is our info-tech center," Den began. "As you might imagine, the readout panels are extensive. Every single aspect of the ship is monitored, from damage control to how our plants are growing in the greenhouses."

"A complex operation," Obi-Wan observed. He gave Anakin a look. He had already briefed his Padawan on what he should do.

While Den continued to talk and Obi-Wan murmured admiring comments or questions, Anakin slipped away. He stood examining a readout console. When he knew Kern was looking at him, he glanced up and caught his eye.

"I've never seen a board like this one," he said.

"It's a big ship." Kern turned away, bored by the prospects of conversation with a young boy.

"Do the readout monitors really capture every single thing that could go wrong?" Anakin asked.

"Yes."

"Are there separate readouts for every engine part?"

"Yes."

"The thrust trace dampers, even?" Anakin pitched his voice high. He had an ability to seem younger than he was.

"Yes," Kern said, exasperation coloring his voice. "Go away, Jedi kid, I'm busy."

"Let's say your power core overheats, but there's no emergency readout on the converters, and the hyperdrive conduits show a steady lightspeed. Would your readout take into account a faulty hydrostatic field connector?"

Kern swiveled in his chair. "You know a lot for a kid."

"Do you know the answer?" Anakin asked.

"I'd check the readout for the hydrostatic field connector, but first I'd investigate the drive turbine air intake," Kern said. "We've got a couple of sublight engines of the Dyne class, and sometimes those flaps can get gunky if the fuel lines get clogged. Okay, kid?"

"Okay," Anakin said cheerfully.

He joined up with Obi-Wan and Den, who was concluding the tour. As soon as they were outside, he repeated the conversation to Obi-Wan.

"I'm telling you, something's up with this guy," Den said. "Readout tech workers are totally separate from motor experts. They don't know about sublight engines. They just send the information to the mechanics."

"He could have worked on engines before," Obi-Wan pointed out.

"But it doesn't say that in his text doc," Den shot back.

Obi-Wan frowned. "I know. Let's go back to my cabin."

It was at times like this that Obi-Wan missed Tahl. When he'd been with Qui-Gon, they could always rely on Tahl to do an exhaustive search, using all her contacts. She inevitably turned up clues that brought them to the next step. And she'd done it fast.

He didn't know Tnani Ikon, the Jedi Knight now in charge of computer searches at the Temple. But Obi-Wan called him and quickly told him that they needed deep research on Kern, sending Tnani all the text-doc information they already had. He asked for priority, but he could never be sure what other Jedi missions were at stake.

Obi-Wan cut the communication but did not put away his comlink.

"What is it?" Anakin asked.

"I have an idea." Obi-Wan contacted Tnani again. "While you're doing the search, can you also investigate any Kerns who have died within the last twenty years?"

The impassive Jedi Knight did not question Obi-Wan. "I will do so."

Obi-Wan cut the communication again. Den looked at him quizzically.

"What was that about? Sure, the guy is ugly, but he doesn't look dead," Den said.

"I'm still thinking about that high security clearance," Obi-Wan said, tucking his comlink back into his utility belt. "I remember that Qui-Gon told me that there are secret operatives called 'no-names' who are used by the Senate. They use fabricated identities that are retired when they die. Except Qui-Gon knew of several cases where if someone had enough money or influence they could buy a retired identity." Obi-Wan shrugged. "Maybe Kern is a purchased identity. It's worth checking into."

"I knew I needed you!" Den said, clapping Obi-Wan on the back.

"But if Kern is a bought identity, that means that somebody powerful wanted him to infiltrate this ship," Anakin said. "Who could it be? And why?"

"That," Obi-Wan said, "just might turn out to be the most important question of all."

CHAPTER 17

Den had to return to his job — "They've got me raising vegetables, can you believe that?" — so while he was waiting for Tnani to reply, Obi-Wan suggested to Anakin that they strike up conversations with some of the residents of the *BioCruiser*.

They spoke to as many beings as they could — a librarian, a tech worker, a teacher, a former ruler of her planet who was now an administrator aboard ship. Each of them spoke glowingly of Uni and their life aboard the *BioCruiser*. Each of them looked at their decision to leave their worlds as a kind of salvation.

"What do you think?" Obi-Wan asked Anakin as they headed to a nearby café for the midday meal. "Do they seem brainwashed to you?" He was always curious about Anakin's perceptions. Often he was startled to discover they were sharper than his own. Anakin saw things intuitively, while Obi-Wan knew he had a tendency to overanalyze.

"Not brainwashed," Anakin said. "Just sad, somehow."

"Sad?"

"Well, they gave up. That's always sad, isn't it? And leaving your family and friends behind makes you sad, too. They push it way down. But it's there. It's there in their dreams. Where else can it go?"

Intrigued, Obi-Wan mulled over Anakin's words. He would not have phrased it that way or perhaps even formed the same thoughts, but Anakin had put his finger on what was bothering him.

The only trouble was, they couldn't bring a charge of "instituting sadness" back to the Senate. They hadn't really found any evidence against Uni.

A group of security officers suddenly wheeled around the corner in lockstep. Obi-Wan watched them curiously at first. Then his instinct kicked in. The officers were coming for the Jedi.

The officers were armed with blasters (still in their holsters) and electro-jabbers (in their hands). Anakin had picked up on the disturbance in the Force a beat later than Obi-Wan.

He tensed and glanced at his Master, uncertain of what to do.

Obi-Wan didn't want to engage with security aboard the vessel. This was to be a peaceful investigation, nothing more.

The lead security officer brandished his electro-jabber. "You must come with us."

"On whose authority?" Obi-Wan asked.

"Uni's. Now move."

The officer raised his electro-jabber and moved toward Anakin. Obi-Wan saw that he meant to use it. Such a blow could paralyze Anakin's arm or leg for some time.

The security officer didn't have a chance to blink. Obi-Wan's lightsaber was activated and moving before the electro-jabber had shifted even a few centimeters. The lightsaber neatly cleaved the jabber in two. The officer crashed to his knees from the strength of the blow. He was unhurt, but dazed.

Immediately the other security officers sprang forward. Anakin had already whirled away from the first officer and drawn his lightsaber. It was only a training lightsaber on loan from the Temple, but even its low power was effective.

"No harm, only disarm," Obi-Wan had a chance to murmur before he flipped backward to avoid a security officer who tried to come at him from his left. Obi-Wan turned, his lightsaber a blur of heat and energy, and turned the electro-jabber into a smoking heap on the floor.

Anakin's training lightsaber circled and whirled before an upward sweep sent the third officer's electro-jabber crashing to the floor in two molten piles. Obi-Wan and Anakin sprang forward to defend themselves against the last two officers, who stumbled backward, un-nerved by the display of Jedi skill. One dropped his electro-jabber and fumbled for his blaster. Obi-Wan cleaved the other's electro-jabber in two and turned the blade of the lightsaber close to the last officer's face.

"Do you really want to draw that weapon?" he asked.

The security officer's eyes wobbled. He licked his lips. "N-no."

"We will come with you voluntarily," Obi-Wan said, looking at each officer in turn. "Do you understand?"

The first officer stood. "We are well trained," he said to Obi-Wan. "We just never met Jedi be-fore. If you'll follow us . . ."

Obi-Wan deactivated his lightsaber and mo-tioned for Anakin to do the same.

The security officers formed a wary guard around them. The first officer marched toward the turbolift.

"What do you think this is about?" Anakin murmured.

"I have no idea," Obi-Wan answered. "Either we've violated some rule, or Uni has decided he's had enough investigation."

They proceeded to the upper level and were marched to Uni's quarters. The doors slid open. The security officers lined up against the back wall. Vox and Uni stood in the middle of the room, waiting for them. Obi-Wan could see that Vox was trembling with rage.

"As always, we see that we cannot trust the Jedi," Vox spat out. "We invited you to share our home, and you have betrayed us. Our confidential files have been broken into!"

Den, Obi-Wan thought in despair. He should have remembered that Den hadn't been the most accomplished thief, even when it had been his profession.

"You are accusing us?" Obi-Wan asked.

"Of course I am accusing you!" Vox almost screamed.

"We did not break into your files," Obi-Wan said honestly.

"Can you tell me you were not involved?" Vox sneered. He waved a hand. "Never mind. My son and I know firsthand how the Jedi order twists the truth —"

"We don't!" Anakin burst out. "Jedi don't lie."

Vox gave Anakin a contemptuous glance. "What do you know, boy? Has your Master told you how he killed another Jedi student and then lied about it? Ah, I thought not."

"That's not true," Anakin shot back.

"The past is not at issue here," Uni said, placing a hand on his father's arm. "We are speaking of right now. You have violated our trust, Obi-Wan Kenobi. We demand that you summon your transport to collect you. Until then, you are confined to your quarters." Uni spoke more calmly than his father, but Obi-Wan could see the hard fury in his eyes. He picked up a sense of triumph as well, as though Uni had been waiting for Obi-Wan to misstep. He was exhilarated to have an excuse to toss the Jedi off his ship. Things were still personal between them.

"I am here on the Senate's behalf," Obi-Wan tried. "If you order us to leave before our investigation is complete, a fuller investigation will follow. The Senate will not take kindly to this, especially since you have no evidence that we were involved."

A flicker of worry passed over Uni's face, but Vox waved his hand as if flapping away a pesky insect. "We are not worried about that," Vox said. "The Senate does not frighten us."

"Contact your return transport right now," Uni said. "We do not allow outsiders to dock on our ship, but we will make an exception. Then we must confiscate your comlink."

Obi-Wan considered his options. They could resist. Escape from this room would be easy. He was not threatened in the least by the security officers in the room, although no doubt Uni and Vox gained comfort from their presence.

But where would they go? They could hide on the ship. Den would help them. But what would that accomplish? He had not seen any evidence that beings aboard the *BioCruiser* were mistreated. There was no compelling reason for him to defy Uni and Vox at this point.

The veiled triumph in Uni's gaze now blazed into life. He had Obi-Wan cornered, and he knew it.

Obi-Wan reached for his comlink and activated it. He punched in Garen's frequency.

"We are done here," he said. "We need a pickup." He gave Garen the coordinates that Uni handed him.

"That was fast. You're lucky. I'm nearby, in the Tentrix system. I can be there in an hour," Garen replied.

They cut the communication. Uni nodded in satisfaction and held out his hand. Obi-Wan put his comlink into it. He then turned to Anakin. After a nod from Obi-Wan, Anakin placed his comlink in Uni's hand.

"These will be returned to you before your departure," Uni said.

"Unlike you, we are not thieves," Vox sneered.

"The security officers will escort you back to your quarters," Uni said. "I will not be seeing you again, Obi-Wan Kenobi." For the first time, he smiled. "I must admit I am glad of it."

CHAPTER 18

Obi-Wan requested that Anakin be allowed to remain with him in his quarters. After a second of hesitation, the first security officer agreed. The door hissed shut, and they were alone.

"Do we really have to leave?" Anakin asked.

"We have an hour," Obi-Wan said. "We should be able to find something out in that time. I wish Uni hadn't asked for our comlinks. We need to hear from Tnani about the background check on Kern."

"But what can we do locked in here?" Anakin asked.

"They didn't take our lightsabers," Obi-Wan pointed out. "I think they knew we would not give them up voluntarily. We can get out if we have to. But I don't think we'll need to cut our way out."

Anakin grinned. "Den?"

Obi-Wan nodded. "I'm sure he'll be along.

Now, what were your conclusions about the meeting?"

Anakin sat on a chair and focused his concentration.

"Vox was afraid," he said at last.

Obi-Wan nodded. "Good."

"It is hard to separate fear from anger," Anakin went on slowly. "Yet I sensed the fear propelling the anger."

"We don't know if he can pinpoint that we were looking for information on Kern," Obi-Wan said. "I have to assume that Den was smart enough to cover his tracks in that area. But he knows we were searching the text-doc files. That was enough to unnerve him. It's a good sign. Den was right. Something *is* wrong here. Anything else?"

"The point where he *should* have been nervous, he wasn't," Anakin said. "Most beings in his situation would worry about the Senate's reaction to kicking two Jedi off the ship. After all, they had no evidence we were involved in the text-doc theft. Uni looked worried. But that seemed the least of Vox's concerns."

"Very good, Padawan," Obi-Wan congratulated him. "I could not ask for a more perceptive reading of the situation."

Anakin gave him a sidelong look. "If I am so perceptive, why don't you trust me?"

Surprised at the blunt question, Obi-Wan sat opposite from Anakin. Memory flooded back. Qui-Gon had kept things from him, too. Now Obi-Wan understood his Master's caution. But he also remembered how Qui-Gon's decision to share his past had deepened their connection. It was what he wanted for himself and Anakin.

It was time to tell his Padawan about Bruck.

He took his time, explaining the Temple sabotage, his history with Bruck, and the agony of seeing a boy he'd known die. He explained the hearing but did not tell Anakin of the guilt he felt. Anakin did not have to know every detail.

Anakin shook his head in disbelief when Obi-Wan had finished. "How could they suspect you?"

Obi-Wan's gaze grew cloudy. "Bruck and I had never gotten along. After his death I wondered if I had been the best Jedi I could have been. Instead of meeting his anger with my own, could I have absorbed it without complaint? Could I have tried to understand the source of it? Would that have changed the course of Bruck's life?"

Obi-Wan's gaze cleared, and he looked at Anakin with his usual keenness. "You see why the Jedi Masters at the Temple often speak to you of anger and fear, Anakin. They have seen what it can do. So have I."

"I have, too," Anakin volunteered. "I was a slave, remember, and the son of a slave? I was not brought up in the Temple surrounded by fountains and peace and gentleness. I think I know better than anyone what fear and anger can do."

Anakin's voice was suddenly harsh. Obi-Wan paused, letting the tone remain in the air between them. "I have not forgotten that, Anakin," he said quietly. "Nor should you. It is part of what shapes you. But if that memory always brings you back to your anger, you must find a way to think of it differently."

A soft knock came at the door. "Are you in there?" Den called softly.

Obi-Wan quickly crossed to the door. "We've been locked in. Can you get us out?"

Den chuckled. "Does a dinko bite? Does a howlrunner howl? Does a nightcrawler —"

"All right, Den," Obi-Wan said through the door. "But first we need a comlink. I have to contact the Temple."

"No problem," Den murmured. "I'll be back before you notice I'm gone. Don't go anywhere."

They heard his footsteps recede.

"Let's get back to Vox Chun," Obi-Wan said. "If we both picked up that it was odd he wasn't nervous about the Senate reaction, we should wonder why."

"I don't know," Anakin confessed.

"There are two possible answers," Obi-Wan said thoughtfully. "One, that Vox has a powerful ally in the Senate who will smooth over any difficulties for the *BioCruiser*. Or two — and this is more disturbing — that Vox is allied with an organization that is even more powerful than the Senate." Obi-Wan stood up and began to wander around the room. "The galaxy has changed. It's full of criminal organizations. Some of them are enormously powerful. With the Senate mired in debate, there is little they have done to control this. Even Chancellor Palpatine is powerless to stop their growth."

"If the second guess is true, do you think this powerful organization is interested in the *BioCruiser*?" Anakin asked.

"Well, it does have a large treasury," Obi-Wan mused. "But attacking a ship this large has logistical problems. They wouldn't want to destroy the ship — they'd lose the treasury. There could be another reason, something else we don't know yet."

They heard a series of beeps at the door, and it slid open. Den jumped inside quickly and the door hissed shut behind him. He tossed Obi-Wan a comlink.

"You see? I can always get you out of trouble," he beamed.

"You got us *into* trouble," Obi-Wan pointed out. "Vox and Uni figured out that someone had broken into the text-doc files."

"Kill me now!" Den said, his hand over his heart. "I did my very best. Nobody's perfect."

Obi-Wan signaled Tnani at the Temple. A moment later his voice came through. "Obi-Wan, I have been trying to signal you. Someone answered but they did not use the coded frequency."

"My comlink was confiscated," Obi-Wan explained. "What do you have?"

"The text-doc for Kern checks out on all the normal channels for deep background," Tnani said. "But a little further digging tells me that Kern is actually a fabricated identity. This being called Kern died eight years ago. Here is the odd thing — he was a Senate operative."

"A no-name," Obi-Wan said.

"Yes, that is the term. Those names are retired, but someone has resurrected this one."

"Thank you, Tnani." Obi-Wan turned to the others. "If Kern is in league with Vox, they must be planning something. And if they suspect that we are close to exposing them, that might step up their timetable."

"Right now there is a General Meeting taking place in the great hall two levels down," Den told them. "Everyone is required to attend, except for skeleton staff. Vox's quarters are empty." He held up the small device he had used to circumvent the door's security system. "I can break in."

Anakin jumped up. "What are we waiting for?"

They met no one as they hurried to Vox's quarters. It only took Den three seconds to break into the room. Vox had plush, comfortable quarters twice the size of Uni's. Obi-Wan, Anakin, and Den searched the room and went through Vox's holofiles. They found nothing suspicious.

"Well, of course he wouldn't leave anything incriminating out in the open," Den said, his gaze roaming the room. "Let's see. Beings usually hide things according to their natures. Vox is vain, lazy — never seen him volunteer to help a soul on this ship — and frail." Den crossed to Vox's sleep-couch and lay down on it experimentally. "You see? Everything is right here, so he doesn't have to get up. Comlink, monitor, light, mirror — I told you he was vain . . ." Den flipped over in order to examine the buttons on a console. "Why are there so many buttons on this thing?"

Den pressed a button, and the closet doors opened. Another, and the light over the washbasin came on. He pressed buttons and levers and dials, activating various doors and lighting controls. He pressed one button and loud music suddenly blared. Anakin covered his ears.

"Glad to see you're keeping this low profile," Obi-Wan shouted over the music as Den fell off the sleep-couch in an attempt to turn the music off.

The music ended abruptly. The silence was complete. Den remained on the floor.

"Den?"

"Well, kill me now. What's this? Another control panel." Den reached out an arm and pressed a button just below the slat of the sleep-couch, where someone lying down could easily reach it.

The thick railing of the sleep-couch support slid out, knocking Den in the head. It revealed a secret drawer cleverly concealed in the bottom of the sleep-couch.

"Ow!" he cried, rubbing his forehead.

Obi-Wan hurried forward. "What is it?"

Den craned his neck to see into the compartment. He let out a low whistle.

"Somebody's not turning over his own wealth to the ship treasury, that's for sure," he said. "Look at all this crystalline vertex. Tradable throughout the galaxy." Den held up his cupped hands, displaying the currency. "Can you imagine his face if he found all this gone?" Den made an approximation of Vox's long, thin face, then added an expression of horror.

"Put it back," Obi-Wan told him sternly.

"Joke, right?" Den asked hopefully.

"May I remind you that you're a *former* thief?" Obi-Wan pointed out.

Den sighed and let the vertex run through his fingers back into the drawer. "Let's try the next button. This time I'll keep my distance." Den jumped up on the sleep-couch for safety this time. He pressed the next button, and another concealed compartment slid out.

Obi-Wan hurried forward. "There's a holoprojector here, too. Now we're getting somewhere." Obi-Wan quickly activated the device, accessing the file directory.

"Let's see," Obi-Wan murmured. "Here's an itinerary of stops the *BioCruiser* will make over the next six months."

"That's odd," Den said. "I didn't think stops were planned in advance. We just cruise until we have a problem, then find the nearest planet. Or at least we're supposed to think so."

"Here's an evacuation plan for the ship." Obi-Wan accessed the file. "It looks pretty routine. But why would Vox be so interested in safety procedures?"

"Beats me. I was on the original committee that drafted the plan. He never came to the meetings. What's that?" Den pointed to an icon at the bottom of the plan. Obi-Wan touched it, and another file opened. It was titled "Broken Circle," but it was blank.

"This could be coded," Den said. "Holofiles can appear blank if you don't know the password. Not to worry, my friends. I never met a code I couldn't crack. I just need a little time." He looked over at a chrono on Vox's table. "We'd better get back. The meeting is over. But let's take this before we go." Den reached down and swept up the tiny holoprojector unit. He stuffed it inside his shirt.

"But Vox will notice that it's missing," Anakin said.

"So what?" Den grinned. "By the time he figures it out, you two will be halfway to Coruscant."

They had started toward the door when Obi-Wan noticed a light flashing on Vox's main control panel. "What's that?"

Den went forward to examine it. "There's a ship approaching the docking bay. Could it be your pickup?"

"If it is, we'd better get back to our quarters," Anakin said . . . just as they heard footsteps outside the door.

CHAPTER 19

Obi-Wan signaled them to retreat toward the closet. He would rather avoid confrontation. It was imperative that they get the holoprojector out so that Den could break the code of that file.

They squeezed inside Vox's huge closet, pressed up against his many fine tunics and robes. Obi-Wan left the door open a tiny crack.

Vox entered the room. He immediately crossed to his sleep-couch. He accessed the hidden drawer with the crystalline vertex. Obi-Wan heard Den let out a muffled groan as Vox scooped it out into a drawstring pouch.

Vox tucked the pouch inside his tunic. He looked around the room for a moment, his eyes taking in the comfortable quarters. Then he hurried out, the door closing behind him.

They eased out of the closet.

"If he's taking all his vertex, something's up," Den said.

"Can you get us to the docking bay to meet Garen without being seen?" Obi-Wan asked. "Another Jedi might come in handy."

"Does a nightcrawler crawl?" Den grinned.

Den knew the unused corridors of the ship, where food and supplies were moved from one area to another. He was able to get them to the docking bay without being seen.

They lingered near the outflow pipes. Garen's sleek starship had landed, and he was checking in with the *BioCruiser*'s technicians.

"If they don't know we're missing, they will soon," Obi-Wan said. "We have to get Garen's attention."

Anakin focused inward. He drew in the Force from all the elements around him. He motioned to Garen and saw the tall young man look up. His gaze roamed around the docking bay and then focused on where they were hiding.

"He knows we're here," Anakin said.

Den gazed at him, baffled. "How did you do that?" He shook his head. "Is it really too late for me to become a Jedi? I could use some of those skills. Not to mention those lightsabers."

"Yes, it's too late," Obi-Wan said, his eyes on Garen.

Garen was now talking in a friendly way with the *BioCruiser* tech worker, gesturing around the giant hangar. Obi-Wan knew that his old friend was complimenting the ship and the design. The tech worker nodded, gesturing at the space, and walked off. Garen began to casually stroll around the hangar, seeming to admire its design.

He came closer and lingered near them. "What's up?"

Obi-Wan spoke in a low voice. "Things have changed. We need you to sneak away and come with us."

"Be happy to." Garen glanced around at the tech workers. They were busy at the console, so he quickly melted back in the shadow of the outflow pipes.

Obi-Wan quickly explained the situation. "We need to investigate what Vox Chun is doing before we leave the ship," he concluded. "I have a feeling the people aboard the *BioCruiser* could be in danger."

Gravely, Garen nodded.

"I've got a place where we can hole up until I break this code," Den told them. "It's not far."

They sneaked back the way they had come. As they reached the utility corridor they had used to enter, suddenly Den sprang back and motioned to them to do the same. "It's Kern," he whispered. "Why is he heading to the docking bay?"

They pressed back into the shadows of the columns supporting the bay. Kern passed them, looking harried.

Garen frowned. "Who is that?"

"We think he might be in league with Vox," Obi-Wan told him. "We don't have proof yet."

Garen nodded, but his expression still seemed absentminded. "He looks . . . familiar."

"Come on," Den urged.

Den led them through a maze of utility corridors to the greenhouse where he raised the native flowers and vegetables of Telos. At the sight of blooming purple flowers, Obi-Wan suddenly remembered a ride on a speeder over the fields and mountains of the Telosian wilderness, so many years ago. They had fought so hard to save Telos. Yet its natural beauties had ended up destroyed. Offworld had started the process, under the name of the company UniFy. Other powerful interests had taken up where Offworld had left off. . . .

Remembrance flooded Obi-Wan. "Broken Circle," he said to Den. "What happened to Offworld after it was kicked off Telos?"

"I suppose they went on to ravage the rest of the galaxy," Den said. "They reorganized under a different name, I heard. They were never allowed to operate on Telos again."

"Xanatos had a scar on his cheek," Obi-Wan

said. "He made it himself by pressing his father's molten ring against his skin. The ring had been broken by Qui-Gon's lightsaber. It was a broken circle."

"Do you think Broken Circle is Offworld?" Garen asked.

"It makes sense," Obi-Wan said. "Vox was secretly in league with Xanatos and Offworld. What if he never broke those ties? And Offworld was used to setting up other companies to conceal their involvement."

"So Vox could have never stopped working for them!" Den said excitedly. "Let me tackle that coded file."

Quickly, Den set up the holoprojector. He used the code "Offworld," and nothing happened.

"Try UniFy," Obi-Wan suggested.

Den typed out the word. "We're in," he said in satisfaction. The others pressed forward to read the file.

"We're right," Obi-Wan said. "These are the records of a mining corporation."

Anakin's face fell. "But this is just a list of planetary operations. That doesn't help us much."

Obi-Wan exchanged a glance with Den. "Unless . . ."

Den nodded grimly. He called up the file that listed the *BioCruiser*'s scheduled stops.

"Each of the stops the *BioCruiser* has made has been to a planet targeted by Offworld for development," Obi-Wan noted. "Vox Chun is always in the landing party."

"And up to no good, I'm sure. Bribes or intimidation, who knows," Den said. "And look how successful he's been. *BioCruiser* shows up at a planet, and a few weeks later they allow Offworld development. It's a beautiful system. Kern is in the readout room. He triggers the need for fuel or repairs. It's not done often enough to cause suspicion. We orbit the planet, and Vox goes down to do Offworld's dirty work. No wonder his secret drawer was filled with crystalline vertex. He probably uses it for bribes."

"Do you think Uni knows?" Anakin asked.

"No way to tell," Den said. "I don't think so, though. I may not agree with Uni, but I don't think he's a crook like his father."

"I don't either," Obi-Wan agreed.

"But why was Kern heading to the docking bay now?" Den wondered. "Is he planning to leave the ship?"

Obi-Wan leaned forward again and studied the list of planets where Offworld had mining operations. "What system are we near now, Garen?" he asked.

"Tentrix," Garen answered. "It's a few hours away."

"That must be TRX. It's the only system that's coded." Obi-Wan accessed the name, and a new file appeared. Once again, they all leaned forward to study it.

After a moment, Den let out a long breath. "Kill me now," he breathed. "I can't believe this. Let me look at those evacuation plans again."

Den activated the evacuation file. He carefully studied the blueprints for long minutes.

"This is different from the official plan," he said finally. "The official plan calls for an escalating series of emergency codes so that we don't panic anyone. We would need organization and control to offload so many beings. This plan calls for an immediate Code Five. That means the vessel is breaking up, and evacuation has to proceed immediately. And the code is instituted in the tech readout room — not the bridge."

"Kern," Anakin said.

"It's clever," Obi-Wan said. "A false Code Five will be instituted. A fake distress signal will be sent. And who will answer it?"

"Offworld ships," Garen said grimly.

"According to the Broken Circle plan, all the beings will be evacuated," Obi-Wan continued. "Offworld droids will board the vessel and remain — only they won't be helping with the rescue effort, they'll be stealing the treasury. Then

Offworld will blow up the *BioCruiser*. None of Uni's followers will realize that the ship was blown up intentionally. Offworld will look heroic, and no one will know it stole the entire treasury."

"How will Offworld blow up the ship?" Anakin asked.

"It must be already set to blow," Den said, his face white. "It's already been sabotaged."

"We did find out that Kern knows his way around a starship engine," Anakin said.

"Kern!" Garen burst out. "I know where I've seen him before. His name was Tarrence Chenati. He sabotaged the Jedi starfighters twelve years ago. He disappeared without a trace."

"And was given a new identity," Obi-Wan said. "Strange that both times Vox has been around, isn't it?"

"Do you think he was behind the sabotage of the starfighters?" Garen asked, his face grim.

"It's a big coincidence if he wasn't," Obi-Wan pointed out. "Vox wanted to discredit the Jedi and distract us —" He frowned. "That reminds me of something Qui-Gon told me when Xanatos was sabotaging the Temple. The keys to destroying something are disruption, demoralization, and distraction." He exchanged a glance with Garen. "Vox wanted to win in that hearing.

He certainly managed to distract and disrupt us. I think we solved the mystery of who was behind the sabotage of your starfighters."

"Can we get back to the present?" Den asked. "Uh, I hate to remind you, but the ship might blow up."

"We must go to see Kad now," Obi-Wan said. "He needs to hear this information. Den, you try to find Kern."

"Do you think Kad will listen?" Anakin asked doubtfully. "You're his worst enemy."

"It doesn't matter," Obi-Wan said. "We have to try."

CHAPTER 20

Kad's face was pale. He was so furious he could barely form words. "How dare you accuse my father of this?"

"We have the holographic files," Obi-Wan said. "And your father has a pouch full of vertex. If you would only look . . ."

Vox Chun sat impassively during the Jedi's denunciation. Now he rose and pointed a shaking finger at them. "Liars and thieves! Nothing has changed, my son."

"Are you so bent on destroying my family?" Kad asked Obi-Wan hoarsely. "Do you hate us so much?"

"It is not hate that brings me here," Obi-Wan said earnestly. "It is justice, and the safety of those you have brought aboard the *BioCruiser*. At any moment, Offworld ships will be surrounding us."

"I assume this is your pilot," Kad said, indicating Garen. "I am ordering you to leave my vessel. You have intruded on my peace for the last time. Go!" He shouted the last word, his pale face suddenly suffused with red.

Just then the announcement system on Kad's console crackled to life. "Attention, attention," a voice said. "Ships are ringing our vessel, claiming they received a distress call. We cannot trace the call. Please advise."

Kad moved his head in increments, as though it was painful for him. At last he locked gazes with his father.

"You have done this?" he croaked.

Vox did not answer.

"Answer me!" His voice was suddenly full of strength.

Vox took a step toward his son. "You can come with me. They will take care of both of us, they promised —"

"No!" Kad covered his ears like a child for a moment, then dropped his hands. "You've betrayed me, you've betrayed my cause —"

"*Your* cause," Vox corrected angrily. "Did I have a choice in the matter? I am an old man."

"Obviously, you have made sure that your own nest is feathered," Kad said scornfully. "Didn't I give you everything you desired? The finest quarters on the ship, the ability to visit other worlds? You had a good life here. You did not need money. Is your greed so ravenous?"

"It is not money I want," Vox answered, drawing his fine cape around him. "It is power. You are right about only one thing in this philosophy of yours, my son. The galaxy is changing. Corruption is everywhere. And I will not be left behind! You have never understood that to be ruthless is to win. I have powerful friends, I always have. Yes, I would stop at nothing to get what I want. I wanted justice twelve years ago. So did you. If I arranged to sabotage a few Jedi starfighters, what of it?"

Kad straightened his shoulders and fixed his father with a steely gaze. "This ends now. I will inform the Offworld ships that the *BioCruiser* is not in danger. Then you may choose a planet, and I will transport you there. I will never see you again."

Vox appeared shaken by his son's cold tone. "I see I must agree." He strode from the room without a backward glance.

Kad turned away from the Jedi for a moment to compose himself. When he turned back, his eyes were clear.

"I had no idea," he said.

"We know that," Obi-Wan told him.

Suddenly, the ship was rocked by an explosion. Kad was thrown to the floor. Obi-Wan and

Garen planted their feet and rode out the blast. Anakin staggered.

The comlink Den had given him signaled. Obi-Wan activated it. Den's agitated voice boomed out.

"Kern has sabotaged the ship! It's breaking apart!"

CHAPTER 21

Obi-Wan, Anakin, and Garen raced to the docking bay. Kad tried to keep up, but lagged behind. When the Jedi reached the docking bay, they saw Den desperately trying to detain both Kern and Vox, who were attempting to access the escape pod. Kern had his blaster drawn. Den was unarmed, and had grabbed a hydrospanner for defense. The attempt was foolish and brave.

Obi-Wan reached out to the Force. He held out a hand and a pile of equipment barrels shot out from a stack and tumbled to the floor between Kern and the pod airlock doors. That should also give Den cover.

Vox grabbed at Kern's arm. "You stole the treasury! That wasn't the plan! What is Offworld going to do with me?"

Kern shook him off and tried to aim at Den. "Get away from me, old man!" He caught sight of the Jedi and turned the blaster fire toward them.

Garen and Obi-Wan deflected the fire as they ran, their lightsabers swinging and circling in a blazing trail. Frail Vox summoned up a burst of strength and dodged around the barrels toward the pod. He accessed the doors and jumped inside the pod.

Kern leaped over the barrels clumsily, keeping up a furious rain of fire at the Jedi. Obi-Wan jumped forward, accessing the Force to cross a great distance. He landed on the opposite side of Den.

With a casual gesture, Kern turned for a split second, shot Vox, then threw him out of the pod. A wounded Vox hit the ground.

"Father!" Kad screamed. He had arrived at the landing bay and now began to rush forward.

Kern aimed his blaster at Kad as he dove backward into the pod. Anakin sprang forward to deflect fire as Obi-Wan lunged for the closing escape pod doors. He was too late. Kern jumped inside, and the escape pod blasted off.

Kad raced to his father's side and fell to his knees. Garen checked Vox's vital signs and shook his head at Obi-Wan. Vox was dying.

The ship reeled from another blast. Tech workers began to rush into the landing bay, trying to ready escape ships. Kad did not notice. He gathered up his dying father in his arms.

Vox's lips were white. "Forgive me, son."

Tears fell like soft rain from Kad's cheeks onto his father's uplifted face. He wiped them away from his father's face with great gentleness.

"Yes, Father," he said. "I forgive you."

Vox barely managed a nod. Then, his gaze still on his son, he died.

Kad bowed his head over his father. Obi-Wan motioned to the others to step back.

"We have to get everyone off the ship," he said. "I've no doubt that if Kern really double-crossed Vox and stole the treasury, he has rigged the ship to explode."

Just then Andra burst in, running toward them at full tilt. Her eyes took in the scene of Kad cradling his father's body. Another explosion sent the ship trembling.

"What's happening?" she asked, her gaze wide and fearful.

"We must evacuate the ship," Den told her. "Kern has sabotaged it."

"We are also under attack," Andra told them. "Those ships that arrived due to a false distress call are now shooting at us. The defensive shield has been sabotaged."

Anakin stepped forward. "We need to fight them from the air."

Obi-Wan knew his Padawan was right. He also knew that Anakin wanted to be a part of that fight. His need to protect Anakin and the knowledge of Anakin's extraordinary skills as a pilot battled inside him. Anakin kept his gaze on Obi-Wan. There was no pleading in it. It was the steady gaze of a Jedi, not a boy.

Obi-Wan turned to Andra. "Do you have a fast attack ship?"

She nodded. "We are peaceful, not stupid."

"Anakin will pilot it."

"I'll use my starship," Garen said. "Come on, Anakin."

"I'll organize the evacuation with Andra," Den said. "There's no time to lose."

Kad rose from the floor. "I'm needed on the bridge. We'll have to find the closest port."

Kad's comlink signaled, and a panicked voice boomed out. "An attack droid team has boarded the ship! They're —"

A burst of blaster fire sounded over the comlink, and the voice was cut off.

CHAPTER 22

"I'll handle the droids," Obi-Wan said. He tucked his lightsaber back into his belt and took off.

He raced down the corridors of the lurching ship. While he ran, his mind clicked over the facts that he knew, searching for what didn't fit. He had learned from Qui-Gon that even in the midst of battle, he must not stop thinking.

Vox had accused Kern of stealing the treasury. If Offworld knew that Kern would steal the treasury before leaving the ship, why would they send droids to board it?

The only answer was that Offworld did not know that the treasury was missing. Either Kern had double-crossed Offworld, or he had been a double agent and had never really worked for them at all.

That was a concern for another time. Obi-Wan guessed that the droids were following the original plan and heading for the tech readout controls, and then for the treasury. He hoped he was right.

He raced into the tech readout room. Two tech workers lay on the floor, stunned from blaster bolts. One remaining worker had taken cover behind a console. The droids marched forward, keeping up a stream of blaster bolts from their chests and hands.

Obi-Wan was on them in a flash. His lightsaber was in constant motion. With attack droids, he did not have to worry about the fine points of strategy. They did not have the split-second timing of a living being. They were relentless, and their firepower was rapid and fierce.

Obi-Wan could have relied on someone to cover his flank, but he took the natural defense of the pillars and consoles of the room for cover. He used long strokes to down two droids at a time. He somersaulted through the air, too fast for a droid to track. He slashed through the head of one droid and wiped out the front control panel of another.

He turned and kicked, sending one droid flying, but another had sneaked up on his flank. Blaster fire burned his arm, but he kept moving, slicing the droid in two.

He was hit, but he didn't know how badly. His

left arm was on fire, and useless. Obi-Wan switched his attack to ground level, bending and then using a fast combination of upward strokes to vanquish the rest of the droids.

He stopped at last. Sweat rolled down his face and soaked his tunic. The floor was littered with droids. He felt dizzy from his wound.

The tech worker who had taken shelter behind a console popped up. Obi-Wan recognized him as a Pho Ph'eahian by his four arms and matted blue fur. "You've been hit."

Obi-Wan winced as he looked at the wound. "It's not bad."

"We have a med kit here. Hang on." The tech worker hurried to bring the kit to Obi-Wan. "I have some medic training, don't worry." Using his four arms, he unwound a bandage at the same time he cleaned the wound, shook bacta on it, offered Obi-Wan a sip of water, and bandaged his arm.

"You should get to the loading bays," Obi-Wan told him when he had finished. "The ship is being evacuated."

"Where is Uni?" the worker asked.

"On the bridge. He won't leave the ship until everyone is safe. And he's hoping to get to a port to save the ship."

"Then I'll stay. He'll need someone in the readout room to monitor the equipment."

Obi-Wan nodded at him, admiring his courage. "What is your name?"

"Rhe Pabs."

"Thank you, Rhe Pabs. I'm heading for the bridge now. I'll tell Uni that you'll remain."

Rhe Pabs nodded. The ship suddenly shook from another blast, and Obi-Wan staggered, his arm slamming against the console. He stifled a cry of surprised pain.

"You should see a real medic," Rhe Pabs said.

"And you should evacuate," Obi-Wan said.

They exchanged a grin, and Obi-Wan raced out the door. The corridor was now crowded with the inhabitants of the *BioCruiser*. Some were carrying belongings, some were panicked, some were just bewildered. Over the speaker system, he could hear Andra's calm voice.

"Panic will delay us. Watch out for your neighbor. Proceed to the loading bays. We have room for all. Safety is our first concern. Help your neighbor."

Obi-Wan dashed through the crowd, heading for the bridge. When he burst in, Kad was sitting at the main controls.

"Do you know how to fly this?" Obi-Wan asked him.

"Yes." Kad's face was taut. "I sent the others to the escape liners. I will not leave the ship."

"The tech readout room is still operational. Rhe Pabs has agreed to remain."

"Good." Kad's eyes searched the skies outside the wraparound cockpit window. "Your Jedi are doing well. Two Offworld ships are down."

Obi-Wan saw Anakin's starfighter zooming in and taking aim at an Offworld battleship whose guns were blazing at the *BioCruiser*. The *BioCruiser* staggered from an explosion. Anakin dived, proton torpedoes firing. Another Offworld ship suddenly peeled off from its attack on the *BioCruiser* and swiveled its gunports toward Anakin's ship.

"I hope your Jedi has eyes in the back of his head," Kad murmured.

Obi-Wan hoped so, too.

In many ways, Anakin felt most comfortable alone in the pilot seat of a starship. There was just him and the ship and the infinite ways he could maneuver.

Although it was recognized at the Jedi Temple that he had gifts as a pilot, he did not get much of a chance to fly. That was why he was so frustrated to learn that if only he could turn back time, he could have been one of Clee Rhara's pilots in the training program.

He knew the Offworld ship was behind him.

He did not have to look. But he did not take evasive action. Not yet. He knew the ship would wait until he was out of range of the attacking Offworld ship. They would not want the wreckage of Anakin's ship to spiral into its neighbor.

At the very last second, he pushed the ship, screaming, to the right, then climbed straight up, flipped over, and came upside down toward the ship at his rear.

"Didn't expect that, did you?" he shouted as he fired his proton torpedoes. The Offworld ship disintegrated into a shower of fire and light. Anakin felt his blood rise with the sight. He knew he should not feel triumph, but he did. He was outgunned by the power of the Offworld ships, but he would never be outmaneuvered.

Garen's voice came over the comm unit. "Two ships heading for the escape liners. I'll take the one on the left."

"Copy that." Anakin dived. The controls felt warm in his hands, even though he knew they weren't. A ship felt alive to him, an organic creature he controlled. He had felt that way since the first day he'd put his hands on the controls of an airship, back when he was a young slave boy with a cantankerous Podracer on Tatooine.

He saw Garen ahead now in his sight line.

Garen swung to his left, and Anakin swung farther to the right. Four Offworld ships were bearing down on the escape liners. He could clearly see the Broken Circle logo on their wings.

Anakin reached out to the Force. He felt at one with the engines. The will of the ship was entwined with his. He even felt entwined with Garen.

The two pushed their engines to the maximum. They zigzagged their way toward the larger ships. The ships saw them coming and turned their barrage of firepower on the two agile starfighters.

"Time to climb," Anakin muttered, easing the controls. The ship zoomed upward and he reversed direction, avoiding a blast to his starboard engine.

He somersaulted and came at one ship from a sideways angle, blasting his torpedoes. He peppered the wing with fire, and then he got lucky. One of the blasts hit the fuel tank. The ship went up in a *whoosh,* sending shock waves toward him. His starfighter danced on the vibrations.

"Good show!" Garen called through the comm unit. "Let's get number two in a pincer movement."

"Copy that. Ready or not . . ." Anakin dived to the left while Garen dived to the right. Torpedoes blasting, they caught the second ship between them. The ship spiraled out, its engines dead.

Anakin was already heading for the third ship. While he'd been engaged, the third ship had managed to damage the wing of the rescue liner. Anakin came at the Offworld ship from above, dropping at top speed as though he would crash into the bridge. At this angle, the ship's guns could not reach him. It swerved, and he followed.

When he had a clear shot, he went for the left engine. Torpedoes blasted, and the engine blew. Limping, the Offworld attack ship headed back to the Offworld cruiser.

Garen had taken care of the last ship. Anakin looked around. The sky was empty of Offworld ships.

"I just spoke to Obi-Wan," Garen said. "He and Kad are staying aboard the *BioCruiser*. Kad wants to make it to Tentrix. The guidance system blew. They need us to escort them."

Anakin could tell by Garen's terse wording that the ship was in deep trouble. He could see it: The ship was listing to one side, and great plumes of smoke were rising from the engines. The *BioCruiser* was a death trap.

The last thing Anakin wanted to do was stay out here while his Master was marooned on a failing vessel. He wanted to be by his Master's side.

But he was a Jedi. He was learning that it meant doing things opposite to his nature. He turned the ship to the right and followed Garen.

"I'm getting a reading that the secondary power cell system is going," Rhe Pabs said. His voice was calm, but Obi-Wan and Kad exchanged a glance. If the secondary power cell system went, the ship would go into catastrophic failure. They would not have time to get to an escape pod.

"Rhe Pabs, it's time for you to go," Kad said, his voice even.

"No sir, I think I'll stick it out here."

Kad gave a sigh of exasperation. "All right, then. Keep us posted." He turned to Obi-Wan. "I'm going to gamble. I could use less power, which might spare the system. But we'd just have to keep the ship operational a longer period of time. Other systems are failing, too. I'm going to increase power so we can reach Tentrix faster."

Obi-Wan nodded. "All right."

Kad turned back to the controls. "This is a good time for you to evacuate."

"I'm staying," Obi-Wan said.

"This is not your fight."

"It is now," Obi-Wan responded.

It was an agonizing journey. The ship controls

were erratic. Warning lights flashed on almost every panel.

Obi-Wan kept his eyes on the ships flanking them. They were so close that he could see Anakin's tense expression, the strain on his face as he tried to smile and give Obi-Wan a thumbs-up.

"Why do you want to save the *BioCruiser* so badly?" Obi-Wan asked Kad.

"Because I invited all those beings to join me," he said grimly. "They left their homes. They have lost their treasury. This is the only thing they have left. I will not lose it."

Garen's voice crackled over the comm unit. "Tentrix dead ahead. Orbiting docking platform will be in position in eight minutes."

"We'll make it," Kad muttered.

Now Obi-Wan could see the vast planet of Tentrix. The docking platform was a small dot in the distance, just a bit larger than a star. As they came closer and the docking platform orbited toward them, it grew larger and larger.

"Almost there," Kad breathed.

Suddenly the comm unit came to life, and Rhe Pubs's agitated voice sputtered out a warning. "Attack droids still on board! I saw them heading for the bridge!"

Obi-Wan whirled around, his lightsaber drawn, just as the doors to the bridge slid open.

A squad of battle droids entered, blasters firing. Blaster fire pinged off the console and thudded into the upholstery of the command benches.

Obi-Wan leaped over the console as two droids took aim at Kad. He deflected the fire with his lightsaber at the same time that he sailed toward the droids. He slashed at one droid's control panel while he kicked out at the other. They both fell with a clatter. He whirled around and sliced the next in two. Diverting blaster fire, he advanced steadily until the droids were cornered, then with one stroke, cut both of them off at the knees. They sank to the floor, still firing, and he sliced off their heads. They rolled together with a clunk and were still.

"Beginning docking procedures," Kad said, his voice shaky. He threw Obi-Wan a grateful look. "We'll make it. Thanks to you."

CHAPTER 23

The sun rose late on Tentrix. After their morning meal, Obi-Wan and Anakin went out on the main docking platform to watch the sun splash the deck with orange and touch the planet below with light. Anakin felt exhilarated. It was a good feeling to be halfway across the galaxy from Coruscant and the Temple, looking down at an unfamiliar planet after a successful mission. For the first time, he felt like a true Jedi.

"I don't care what Yoda says," Anakin remarked. "I think discovering sabotage, helping an evacuation, and guiding a crippled ship to safety counts as a mission."

Obi-Wan smiled. "It *was* a mission, Anakin."

"Good," Anakin said with satisfaction. "There are some things I don't understand about it, though."

"That is usually the case after a mission."

"How could Kad forgive his father at the

end?" Anakin burst out. "He had betrayed him. He could have been responsible for countless deaths."

"Yes, he did many bad things," Obi-Wan agreed. "But he asked his son for forgiveness when he was dying. There must have been good in him. I think it is a mark of Kad's character that he was able to forgive his father."

Anakin shook his head. "I still don't understand it."

"Would you forgive Yoda if he did something terrible?" Obi-Wan asked.

"Yoda would never do something terrible," Anakin said firmly.

"No, I don't think he would," Obi-Wan said. "But you must remember always, Anakin, the strength of the dark side."

Anakin's mouth set in a thin line. He still did not understand. He decided to change the subject. "I just wish we'd been able to track Kern."

"Perhaps Garen will be able to." Garen had volunteered to search for the escape pod. They continued to have hope that the *BioCruiser* treasury could be returned.

"I don't understand what Kern was doing," Anakin said. "Was he working for Offworld or not?"

"I doubt it," Obi-Wan said. "I think he is working for a different gang. Or maybe Vox contacted him on Offworld's behalf and he decided to work for himself instead. That treasury was a great temptation. And Kad told me that Kern stole the blueprints of the *BioCruiser*. He has detailed plans of all their technological innovations."

"What do you think he wants with them?"

"He will sell them," Obi-Wan said. "A constantly traveling ship with a large population could be seen as a threat by an organization that seeks control of the galaxy. Whatever or whoever is guiding Kern was interested in destroying Kad's movements as well as stealing the treasury. If we can find Kern, maybe we can get some answers."

"You sound as though you don't think Garen will find him," Anakin guessed.

Obi-Wan looked out at the stars, which were beginning to fade due to the rising sun. "There are many places to hide in the galaxy. And Kern is used to deception. But it is a good ending for your first mission, Anakin. Sometimes evil beings escape. We do what we can."

"But I always want to win," Anakin said.

Obi-Wan frowned. "Missions are not about winning and losing. They are about leaving good behind."

They heard footsteps behind them. Kad came toward them.

"A beautiful world, Tentrix," he said, looking down at the blue planet.

"Will you stay here for a while?" Obi-Wan asked.

"The repairs will take some time, I'm afraid," Kad answered. "We are holding meetings to decide on our next step. It is not clear what that will be. I am reluctant to make the decision. Some talk of colonizing a new world or finding a planet in the Outer Rim that would welcome us. We shall see. I have led all these beings away from what they knew, but I cannot provide them with a future."

"I'm sure the path will become clear," Obi-Wan said.

Kad nodded. "I want you to know that if I am uncertain about the future, I have at least buried my past. I hope it is buried for you, too. You saved my life, but that is not why I can bury it. I know now that you didn't cause my brother's death. Bitterness was at our family's core. I know now that Bruck had it. My father had it. And the hardest thing I had to acknowledge is that I have it, too. I have based a system on rejection. I turned my face away from life. What else causes that other than a bitter heart? Funny how facing that has brought me peace at last."

Anakin watched carefully. His Master and Kad locked eyes. Something passed between them.

He felt something ease in his Master, some heaviness lift from him.

"Then life has given you a gift," Obi-Wan said. "You get to begin again."

"I hear you have arranged transport back to Coruscant," Kad said. "Will you come and say good-bye to Andra and Den? They're waiting for you."

"Of course," Obi-Wan said. "Anakin?"

"I'll be right behind you," Anakin said. He did not want to leave the loading platform just yet. His mind still teemed with questions and lessons. He longed to ask Obi-Wan, but he didn't think he would.

Whatever was in Obi-Wan's past was a wound that went deep. He understood that. He had his own wounds. Maybe someday he would stand as a man, just like Obi-Wan, and feel the burden lift.

He thought again of Kad, cradling his father as he died, tears falling from his eyes. There were levels to compassion he still did not understand. How did a being go about transforming anger into mercy?

Frustration bit inside him. Obi-Wan *tried* to understand him. He loved his Master for that. But no one could understand. Not his fellow students at the Temple, not his teachers, not even Yoda, who seemed to understand so much. Would he always feel apart from the others because of his background? And would that feeling of separation mean that he would never become as great a Knight as Qui-Gon or Obi-Wan? It was his greatest fear.

Anakin turned back toward the shelter of the spaceport, toward friends, warmth, light, and his Master. The future would come, he told himself. At that moment, all he felt was grateful that he had Obi-Wan to show him the way.